# Mystery of the Jungle Airstrip

*Also by Elinor Chamberlain*

MYSTERY OF THE MOVING ISLAND

# Mystery of the Jungle Airstrip

## Elinor Chamberlain

**J. B. Lippincott Company**

*Philadelphia and New York*

# ❀ Contents ❀

# Contents

# 1

# New Base Camp for Ronnie

Ronnie could not sleep.

It was ten minutes past two in the morning, Philippine Time. It was also about ten minutes past two by New York Daylight Saving Time. But in New York it was yesterday afternoon.

Now, right now, in the middle of the night, it was yesterday afternoon.

It was a crazy idea that belonged in a dream. But she wasn't dreaming. She was wide-awake. She yawned, but the yawn was as unreal as the time, whichever time it was.

She was wide-awake in a strange bed in a strange house.

Through the mosquito net she could see only the wide square luminous space that was her window and the small round luminous dial of her clock.

She heard the rustle of wind in coconut palms and the rattle of the thick leaves of banana trees.

Bananas. Were they trees, or were they plants?

They were fruit and she was hungry. There was a big bowl of them on the buffet in the dining room. There were tiny yellow ones and fat red ones and long green ones that were ripe in spite of being green. Her Uncle Frank had eaten one. She remembered now that it had smelled wonderfully good.

She was hungry and she was wide-awake. It was a quarter past two——

No! It was still only ten past two. And the clock hadn't stopped. She could hear the tick.

She might lie awake for endless hours, thinking of food, but one banana would probably put her to sleep in three minutes.

Although she was a stranger, she was one of the family. Her Aunt Pacita had told her that she must feel at home. If she didn't, it was foolish of her. Her uncle and aunt had been very quiet at dinner. They had seemed hardly to know that she was there. But when they did notice her, they were kind enough. It was ridiculous for her not to behave exactly as if she had been here six weeks instead of six hours.

The mosquito net enclosing her bed and tucked carefully under her mattress was a guard against lizards and giant spiders as well as mosquitoes and other insects. She knew this. Nevertheless she suddenly found herself outside the net. Fortunately she had put her bare feet on nothing that crawled, but merely on the cool bare floor.

She went to the window and looked out.

The house was near a hilltop and she was on the second floor. There was a broad verandah running all around this floor and there were wide overhanging eaves. She could not see anything but a sky of clouds and stars.

She turned to the door.

It opened on a short corridor between the verandah and the living room. There, surprisingly, shone a faint yellow light. She felt that it must come from the dining room, as if the bananas were sending it out to guide her.

The floor of the corridor was of smooth, cold, gleaming, dark red tile.

The floor of the living room, or the *sala*, as they called it, was of dark wood, also gleaming but not quite so cold.

And the light was indeed coming from the dining room. Strangely, a direct beam touched a pair of pictures on the wall across the sala. They were pictures of her grandfather and her grandmother, framed differently but otherwise exactly the same as pictures in her mother's New York apartment.

They were like an invitation. They said, "Feel at home, Ronnie, and help yourself to the bananas."

She crossed to the archway into the dining room and stopped with a gasp. Someone was sitting at the table.

He looked up and she recognized him from photographs she had seen. It was her mother's youngest brother, Charles. He said, in surprise and softly, as if to himself, "Well! Sleepwalking?" Then more loudly he said, "No. Awake. You must be Ronnie."

"Yes," Ronnie said. His silence then was like a question, and she added hurriedly, as if in answer, "I'm hungry." She was ashamed of her voice, which suddenly sounded high and childish.

"Hungry?" Charles said. "So am I, now that I think of it." He turned his head to see what she was looking at. "Bananas? I don't think I'm going to be satisfied with just a banana. A sandwich or two and some milk—how about it?" He stood up.

"It would be wonderful." This time her voice was all right.

"Then follow me."

Behind him she crossed the dining room and the verandah and went down the stairs to the verandah below and then into the kitchen.

"My sister-in-law is very proud of this kitchen," Charles said, turning on the light. "All electric. There aren't many such kitchens in the provinces far from Manila." He opened the big refrigerator door and looked inside. "And the cook is proud of it, too. He keeps it as neat as an operating room." He took out bread and butter and handed them to her. "So we must leave no traces. Plates and glasses in the cupboard over to my left, Ronnie. Knives on the rack near the sink—you can see them. Mustard in the cupboard above the knives."

By the time she brought the mustard to the table, he was slicing ham. He said, "I'm good at making sandwiches."

She said, "I'm good at cleaning up."

He put a sandwich on a plate and pushed it toward her. "Sit down," he said, "and get started. I'll catch up. Don't worry about that."

She was glad to obey. The smell of the ham had actually made her feel weak.

As she ate, she watched Charles.

Charles was thirty-two. Her mother was thirty-eight

and her Uncle Frank was forty-seven. There were another sister and two brothers at ages in between; she had met one of her uncles in Hawaii two days before when her plane stopped there.

Charles was good-looking but not handsome. His eyes were like her mother's, large and gray, set wide apart. His curly hair, light to begin with, was sun-bleached besides. His shoulders and arms were thick, but with muscle and not fat. She couldn't call him tall and she couldn't call him short; she would have to say that his height was medium.

But medium was a word that did not suit any of the Richardsons. They were calmer than most people; more alive but more controlled. She thought that if, not knowing them, she had seen any of them in a crowd, they would have stood out and she would have picked them at once as the people she most wanted to know.

Charles was eating now and talking with his mouth full, talking about kitchens and cooks and cooking and food. Delicious words hovered around her: kalamansi, makapuno, chico, lapu-lapu, mango, lechón, papaya, mangosteen, pomelo, lanzón, pancit. Some were familiar, more were not, but all sounded good. She closed her eyes in pleasure.

"Ronnie! Miss Veronica Stewart! Are you falling asleep?"

"No. I'm just enjoying myself. Talk some more about eating. Every word tastes wonderful. And this sandwich——!" She put the last bite in her mouth and reached out for more.

She was still not sleepy when the sandwiches were gone and the kitchen was neat again. Was Charles going to sit up longer? Would he send her back to bed? He had been fun, talking about food all the time, but now she wished he had talked also about something else. There was too much that she didn't know about him, and about her Uncle Frank, and her Aunt Pacita, and her two cousins. She was curious about all of them, and curious, too, about how she was going to spend her time here.

She decided, following him up the stairs, that although her stomach was full, it wasn't too full to hold a banana. That would delay her return to her room. If Charles sat down again at the table . . .

Charles sat down again at the table.

Ronnie went to the buffet, got a banana, sat down at the table opposite him, and began peeling back the thick red skin.

Charles made no comment at all. In fact, he seemed to have forgotten her.

On the table in front of him were two or three dozen colored snapshots, some in piles and some spread out under a strong, small light. He was examining them through a magnifying glass, looking at some over and over again, concentrating intently. He did not once look up at her.

She finished the banana, got up, and returned, though without much inner enthusiasm, to the fruit bowl.

"Are you always so hungry?" said Charles. "Didn't you have any dinner?"

"Dinner was ready when we got here. But after the plane, after the change in time, I didn't feel very hungry. I guess I was too excited."

"Didn't Doña Paz notice that you weren't eating?"

"Who?"

"Your aunt. Doña Paz. You might as well call her that. Everybody does. And just call me Charles. Skip the uncle part."

"Do my cousins call you Charles?"

"They do."

"I suppose I'll meet them next weekend? I suppose their vacation is over? Are they at school in Baguio?"

"Doña Paz and Frank didn't tell you anything?"

"Well, actually," Ronnie said, "they didn't talk very much. A little about my trip, and about my mother's plans for coming here next month, and about how I should feel at home."

Charles leaned back and looked at her. "They should have told you. There's only one thing in their minds right now. Talking about it doesn't do much good. And I suppose they didn't want to spoil your arrival. They didn't realize that they might spoil it by seeming so cold and distant, as if they weren't interested in you. Did you feel that?"

"Well, not exactly——"

"But you must have felt something of the sort. Believe me, they are not acting like themselves." He paused, then said abruptly, "Your Cousin Rafael has disappeared."

"Disappeared? What do you mean?"

"I mean exactly what I said. Disappeared. Disappeared! And now you know as much about it as any of us do. We don't know where he is, or what happened, or why, or if he's alive, or——" He stopped abruptly. After a moment he added, "It's not as if he were a small child. It's a different sort of thing. He's older than you are."

"Three years older," Ronnie said. "When did it happen?"

"Saturday. Sometime Saturday."

"That was the day after I left. And this is Tuesday. No, Wednesday. He's been gone four days."

Charles said, "It seems like four years. And that's why I can't sleep tonight. That's why I was out here—Ronnie, how are your eyes? Do you wear glasses?"

"No."

"Then forget the banana that I know you don't really want, and sit down beside me and tell me what you see in these pictures." He pushed a magnifying glass and a snapshot toward her.

She looked through the glass at the snapshot and then at several more. They were almost exactly alike, and she could not have found top or bottom except for a row of numbers at one edge. She said, "I don't see anything but the tops of trees, taken from a plane, your plane, I suppose. What is it? Jungle?"

"Jungle or mountain forest, whichever you like to call it. I was testing a secondhand camera I just bought and using up some old film. I wanted to see how the machinery worked, for taking pictures in a series. I didn't expect the pictures to be good, but they're perfect. Here are some more. Same series but a little different. Tell me what you see."

"There's a beach across the corner of this one. I see waves. They look like a lace edge between the jungle and the ocean. Is it the ocean? Or is it the China Sea?"

"It's the Pacific."

"And there's a valley with a brown shiny satin ribbon at the bottom. A muddy river?"

"Right."

"And in this one not far from the river there's a light greenish yellowish streak. A muddy green river?"

"Such things exist, but I think not here. Look at the next picture."

"The brown river curves like a snake, but the green streak is straight and it isn't shiny. It isn't water."

"Here," he said. "Use two glasses together. Where did that other one go?" He pushed an envelope aside and found a second magnifier. "Hold one in each hand, and then move them around until you get the right focus. I'll hold the picture flat. I hurried these prints and that makes them curl."

Ronnie understood that for some reason this picture was very important. The others had been preparation. This was the one that mattered. She moved the two glasses carefully and suddenly new details leaped into view.

"Tell me what you see," Charles repeated.

"I see the trunks of the trees along one side of the green streak. And that green looks like grass, nice soft grass."

"It's grass," Charles said, "but it's not soft. Keep on looking."

"Isn't it funny to find a patch of grass in the middle of the jungle?"

"No," Charles said. "Wild people burn patches of jungle to make clearings where they can plant rice. And then this grass takes over, and they move on to another place and burn another clearing."

"Wild people?" Ronnie said. "They must be very clever. How did they ever burn a long patch like this with such straight edges?"

"Good girl!" Charles exclaimed. "That's thinking! But keep on looking, too."

Again Ronnie's eye traveled along the edge of the grass. This time it stopped at something she had let it pass over before. There was a bright mark. She had thought it was a flaw in the film. She reached for the two other pictures that showed the grassy patch, and under the double magnification found the same mark. It was not a flaw.

She said, "Is this bright mark what you wanted me to find? It's about as big as the point of a needle."

"I know. I've looked at it so hard that sometimes I can't see it at all. Thanks, Ronnie. Frank's eyes aren't good enough, and I didn't want to bother Doña Paz with it. I wouldn't bother with it now myself, except that, having found it, I must. That bright spot, Ronnie, is metal reflecting the sun."

"An old tin can?" Ronnie suggested.

"Even an old tin can in that spot would be something to investigate. Though an old one would be too rusty to show. But this is no can. It is above the ground. Look again."

She looked and saw that Charles was right. She said, "It's something sticking out from the jungle like a nose."

Charles took her hand and shook it. "I'm proud to have you for my niece. Now can you tell me what kind of a nose?" When she shook her head, he continued, "You didn't notice, but there's a stretch of jungle there where you can't see any tree trunks along the edge. I think that nose is the nose of an airplane, hidden under the trees. And that grass is an airstrip. And in the jungle in those mountains, they ought not to be. I don't believe it even now, when you see the same thing."

"But it will have to be investigated?"

"Oh, yes. That's the next order of business after we find Rafael."

"Rafael," Ronnie began, and stopped, not knowing what she wanted to say. Realization had been slow in coming to her. Of course she understood Charles's words: Rafael had disappeared. But the feeling of that disappearance had not reached her at once. Now she was feeling it. Now she was beginning to know the emptiness the family knew and the fears they fought off and the hopes they hardly dared to encourage.

Rafael had been there Saturday. Now he was gone. He might be anywhere. He might be nowhere—alive.

Charles repeated, "I'm proud of you. You're now my favorite niece."

"I'm the only one you know," Ronnie said.

"That's true, but how did you guess it?"

"I didn't have to guess. I've been learning about all the Richardsons ever since I was born."

"Your mother has told you a lot about these islands?"

"Of course. I feel almost as if I've lived here before."

"There must be places you want to see, things you want to do. We'll have to make a list."

"It will begin like your list," Ronnie said. "I'm a Richardson, too. My middle name is Richardson. Rafael—Rafael is at the top of the list. Next is that place in your pictures. And I guess that's a long enough list for a while."

"I see." He stood up and put his hand on her shoulder. "You are my favorite niece permanently. Now, back to bed. I think I'll try to sleep, too. You go first, and then I'll turn out the light."

# * 2 *

# *Mission:*
# *Information*

She had expected to lie awake the rest of the night, but she had fallen asleep at once and had slept so hard that when she waked she didn't know where she was. The white mosquito net was like a cage. She sat up staring at it wildly—and remembered. This was Topside, her Uncle Frank Richardson's house, a hundred and fifty kilometers north of Manila, in the Philippines.

She pulled an edge of the net from under the mattress, and stood up and stretched. It was half-past ten. It was hot. Her pajamas were damp across the back.

Inside her room it was dim. Outside it was very bright. She went to the window. Sunlight flashed on palm fronds as the wind tossed them. There were mountains, blue-green, not very far away. She ought to know the name of them. Caballos? Caraballos? Caraballos sounded better.

When she returned from the shower, a Filipino girl in a white dress was tucking the mosquito net up and into itself, so that it hung from the bedposts like a hammock.

"Good morning," the girl said. "I am Teresita." She reached for Ronnie's pajamas. "I take. I wash." She looked around the room. "You have more? This?"

It was the dress in which Ronnie had arrived. She hesitated.

"I can do," Teresita said. "Better all clean. When typhoons come, better all clean, or spots come."

"I know," Ronnie said. "Mildew."

Teresita nodded. She gave another smoothing touch to Ronnie's bed, and hurried away with the clothes to wash them.

Ronnie, brushing her hair, thought about Teresita, old Engracia, and Doña Paz. They were all Filipinos, the first Ronnie had ever met, although she had heard about Doña Paz and Engracia for years. Engracia was Ronnie's mother's old nurse; she had wept last night when she helped Ronnie unpack and she had wept when she tucked in the mosquito net. She spoke very little English, but tears are a language, too. An international language, Ronnie thought, and she had almost answered in tears.

She rather dreaded meeting Engracia this morning.

She also rather dreaded meeting her aunt, Doña Paz, although she was very curious about her. But Doña Paz's thoughts would all be centered on Rafael, and Ronnie would want to speak of him but wouldn't know how to do it.

However, when she finished dressing and left her room, she met only Engracia, and fortunately Engracia this morning was smiling. By daylight she looked a hundred years old and had a thousand wrinkles and one front tooth was missing, but her smile was sweet. She said, "Comb, Berroneeca. Vrrepas."

Veronica understood what she meant: "Come, Veronica. Breakfast."

Ronnie followed her, as she had followed Charles, down the stairs and into the kitchen.

There was a marvelous smell of fresh bread. The cook was taking a pan of rolls out of the oven. He turned and looked at Ronnie, scowling. He wasn't fat and comfortable-looking, as Ronnie thought cooks should be. He was tall and thin, with horn-rimmed spectacles, and he seemed quite young. His skin was much lighter than Engracia's or Teresita's. Ronnie remembered that Charles had said he was Chinese.

"Shoo!" Engracia said, waving a hand in his direction. This, Ronnie learned later, was a sort of introduction. Engracia had spoken the cook's name, which was Hsu.

His scowl did not bother Engracia. Swiftly she plucked two rolls from the pan and dropped them on a plate. She motioned to Ronnie to sit down at the table, put the plate before her, and got butter and milk and marmalade and orange juice from the refrigerator. Then she gave Ronnie another smile, and departed.

Ronnie began to eat.

If the cook glanced toward her, their eyes never met. Whenever Ronnie looked toward him, he was intent on his mixing and stirring. Without the scowl his face had no expression at all. It was easy to understand how a cook so good—the rolls were delicious—with a face so hard to read, except when it was scowling, could become a tyrant in the kitchen. She hoped she had left everything clean enough to suit him when he entered the kitchen this morning.

She finished eating just as Engracia returned and solved the problem of the dirty dishes by motioning to Ronnie to go upstairs again.

Ronnie went up to the sala.

She was apparently alone in the house with the servants. What should she do with her empty time? She might explore the house, wherever she could explore without intruding. But she could not go into her cousins' rooms, or Charles's, which were on one side of the sala, or her aunt's and uncle's room, which with her own room and a vacant bedroom was on the other side. That left only the sala.

There was a grand piano; Doña Paz was a musician. There were newspapers and magazines, some in English, some in a language she could not read, some she knew and more she did not know. There were bookshelves filled with books. There were two sofas and there were big chairs, all of bamboo or something like it, with big cushions; they would be comfortable and cool. But she did not feel like sitting down and reading.

She remembered a pair of photographs she had noticed the night before, facing each other in a folding frame. Where were they? She discovered them at last on a table in a corner, not so easily seen now that the lamp beside them didn't light them. She picked them up and carried them to the wide archway opening on the verandah, where she could see them better.

Her cousins, Rafael and Manuel, looked straight at her. But really, Ronnie thought, that was merely straight at the camera. And what good were pictures, actually, to tell you about people that you didn't know? Or people that you did know? The glass was like a wall . . .

She carried the pictures back and set them down, bending for another look at them.

The two brothers were alike, but Rafael seemed more serious. That was right. He was older. Manuel was even younger than she was herself. Only a boy, Ronnie thought, while Rafael was practically a man. Rafael looked like a person who could take care of himself. But sometimes even the strongest can't take care of themselves.

She had suddenly the uneasy feeling that eyes were looking at her back. Slowly she straightened up, and slowly began to turn.

There was a man silhouetted in the archway. He said, "Who are——? Oh, you must be my Cousin Veronica."

Ronnie's heart leaped. Rafael had come back!

He said, "I didn't mean to frighten you." He pointed to his shoes. "These rubber soles. I'm always making my mother jump, too." He came into the sala. "Where is she? I'd better find her quickly and explain."

"You certainly should find her quickly and explain," Ronnie said. "But I don't know where she——" And then she realized that this wasn't Rafael she was talking to, but Manuel. She said, "I thought you were Rafael."

"Rafael. Is he——?"

She shook her head. "I haven't heard anything. I don't know if there's any news." She added, "You *are* Manuel? You're about three inches taller than me!"

"Whose fault is that?" he said, grinning. But the grin was gone almost as soon as it appeared. "Yes, I'm

Manuel. Usually called Manoling. And my mother isn't here?"

"I haven't seen anybody since I got up but Teresita and Engracia and the cook."

He said, "I'll find Engracia. She'll know where my mother is." He crossed the sala and the dining room, and when Ronnie, following, reached the verandah on that side of the house he was already downstairs, shouting for Engracia.

A few moments later he was at the foot of the stairs shouting, "Veronica!"

"What?" she said, leaning over the railing. "And call me Ronnie, please."

"Can you ride a motorbike?"

"A motorbike! I don't know. I never tried."

"All you have to do is hang on to me. Want to try?"

"Why not? Where are we going?"

"I'll tell you in a couple of minutes. I must change my clothes. And you'll need some dark glasses. Change your clothes, too, if you want to. I'll meet you at the garage."

The garage was a separate building, a short distance down the hill. He was waiting outside with the motorcycle when she arrived. "I think you'd better start riding on level ground," he said. "So we'll walk down to the road and I'll explain while we go. This isn't a sightseeing trip. It's something I want to do. Something that I think has to be done. And I think you can help me." He paused.

"Well?" She looked at him, but he was looking down at the ground as he walked along. "I'm listening."

He raised his eyes and she could see the appeal in them. He did need her for something, and whatever it was, it was important.

"Manoling, if you want me to help you, I'll do anything I can." Then suddenly she understood part of what was in his mind. "Is it about your brother?"

He nodded.

She repeated, "I'll do anything I can to help. Tell me what you want."

"I haven't got it all worked out," he said. "But to begin with, this is my brother's bike. How much do you know about what happened to Rafe?"

"Practically nothing."

"We don't know much more. But the last time we saw him, he was riding on this bike away from the house."

"And it came back? And he didn't?" She looked it over carefully. "It seems to be all right. It isn't smashed up anywhere."

"The P.C.—that's the Philippine Constabulary—found it seventy or eighty kilometers north of here beside a road in the Cagayan Valley. Just lying there. With plenty of gas in the tank."

"But Rafael—wasn't there any trace of him?"

"No. And for a good reason. I don't think he was ever there. But will anybody listen to me? No. I'm just a kid. I don't know anything. So if they won't listen or do anything, that means I have to do it myself, doesn't it? I couldn't stay at school. I took the first ride I could get down from Baguio."

They had reached the road. He put a leg over the motorbike, saying, "I'll tell you more later. All you have to do now is get on and hang on."

Ronnie got on. Manoling started the motor. She hung on, and they went roaring down a narrow gravel road.

# ❄ *3* ❄

# *Small-Unit*

# *Action*

They walked with the motorbike between them along the road, which here was the main street of a village.

"You said it wouldn't be a sightseeing trip," Ronnie said. "But I'm seeing sights. Of course I've seen plenty of sugarcane and coconut palms before, but I never saw a little town like this. What did you say it was?"

"It's called Kabundokan. And it's a *barrio*. You came through plenty of barrios last night driving up from Manila."

"It was dark. I didn't notice houses on stilts, like these, with a ladder up to the door. The roofs are palm leaves, aren't they? And the walls, too."

"Some of them. Some are woven split bamboo. That's called *sawali*, if you want to know the name for it."

"O.K.," Ronnie said. "But that's two new words and

two are enough for now. Do you see how everybody is staring? The children in that yard, and under that house. And see there? Someone is leaning out a window to get a good look at us."

"At *you*. They're sightseeing, too," Manoling said. "Ronnie, are you thinking about what I asked you to do?"

"I'm gradually going nutty over it. I don't know how I can do it."

"I went into the shop Monday morning and I know she saw me, but she pretended she didn't, and she disappeared. When I asked for her, her sister couldn't find her. But if I can get her outside, so I can ask her a few questions—you'll think of a way to do it. I know you will."

Ronnie shook her head, but not really in answer to him. It was a worried shake.

"You're a stranger," Manoling said. "She'll never suspect anything. You want to help me, don't you?"

She nodded her head vigorously, and this time she was answering him, but then she shook it again in doubt. She knew how serious Manoling was and how important this was to him. They had just gone into the church, and he had prayed about it. Standing near the door, in the cool, dim emptiness of the old stone building, she had watched him with astonishment. She had never before seen a boy kneel and pray for something. He could have done nothing else that would have impressed her as much. And she knew that he had not been thinking of impressing her.

"You'll think of a way to do it," Manoling said again.

"You've said that at least ten times!"

"I can't say it much more. We're almost there."

Ahead of them was a row of one-story buildings of whitewashed cement. "It's the sari-sari shop, the first door you come to. I'm going to wait behind that truck that's parked there at the side."

"The *what* shop? No, never mind. No more words like that. Her name is Celia. And it's her father's shop and his name is Lee, only it's spelled *L-i*."

"You aren't supposed to know their names. You don't need to, anyhow."

"Celia has a sister, and you don't want the sister. Celia is the pretty one with dimples."

"That's right. And here's where I stop."

Ronnie walked on alone. She was very warm and the sun shone almost straight down on her, but she shivered a little. Her steps slowed. She didn't know what she could do inside the shop, but that hardly mattered, for she didn't think her legs would carry her into it.

From behind the truck came the words: "Don't be chicken!"

The expression always made her furious. Until this time it had always made her stop at once whatever it was that she was hesitating about. She refused to react childishly to a dare.

But this time she knew she had to continue. That knowledge plus her anger carried her into the little shop.

Everything in the world must be for sale here, she thought. The crowded confusion was like a threat, as if everything, stacks of canned goods, bolts of cloth, heaps of things she couldn't identify, bright shirts hanging from a bar, racks of scissors and needles and pins and gadgets, piles of notebooks and paper, cases of pencils and pens, and more things, and more, were all leaning over her ready to fall and crush her. She blinked her eyes, took a deep breath, and looked again.

There was a tiny open counter and behind it stood a very pretty girl. She smiled at Ronnie and Ronnie saw dimples. Her black hair was short and wavy, held back from her face by a pink ribbon that matched her neat, pink, American-style dress. She said in English, "Can I help you?"

Ronnie smiled and said, "Yes, I think so. I hope so. I need a ribbon like the one you're wearing." The words came out of her mouth as easily as if her plan had not just been born. She gazed at rolls and rolls of ribbons on a shelf behind Celia's head. "How much do I need?"

"One meter and one-tenth," Celia said. She turned to the shelf. "Pink? Like mine?"

"Maybe," Ronnie said. "May I see it? And that deeper pink?"

Celia took down the two rolls.

"Or I might like blue," Ronnie said. "That light blue is pretty. And that dark blue."

Celia took down two more rolls.

"And that blue that's almost green. And that green that's almost blue. And those two greens. And that orchid."

Now there were nine rolls.

"They're all so pretty," Ronnie said, "that it's not easy to choose."

"But one ribbon is never enough," Celia said. "You need for different dresses. And to have a fresh one you need more than one of each color."

"Yes, of course," Ronnie said. "Now, there's something outside that I'd like to match." She picked up the green ribbons. "You bring the blue ribbons and come with me and help me decide."

It took a moment for Celia to agree, but she could not let Ronnie walk out of the shop with ribbons, perhaps not to return. She called, "Pepita, Pepita!" toward a curtain at the back of the shop, and then followed Ronnie.

Around the truck Ronnie went and around the truck came Celia behind her. And that brought her face to face with Manoling.

She could not escape. Ronnie now slipped behind her and she was penned in.

The talk that began then sounded to Ronnie as rapid as a machine gun. How could anyone, she wondered, ever learn such a language? And it was unfair that, after she had arranged this meeting, she couldn't understand a word. Leaning against the truck, she watched their expressions and listened for the changing tones of voice, trying to guess what was being said.

She could see that Celia was frightened. She could see that Manoling's questions were not getting satisfactory answers. She could see that the more he insisted, the more stubborn Celia became. When tears began to run down Celia's cheeks, he gave up. He said in English, "You never liked him, or you'd help me now."

"I don't know where he is, I don't know what happened!" she said. There was pain in her cry, although her voice was hushed, and it went to Ronnie's heart.

There was a little silence, and Celia took out a handkerchief and dried her eyes. Then she said coldly to Ronnie, "Give me the ribbons. You don't like any of the colors. I understand that."

Ronnie had been ready to buy a piece of each color to show her sympathy, but her sympathy died quickly. She stepped forward and put the bright rolls she held into Celia's hands. As she moved there was a sharp sound. Her shorts had caught on a break in the fender against which she had rested, and, reaching back, she found a big three-cornered tear.

Celia saw it. She gave a little sniff that was partly a laugh, shrugged, tossed her head, and walked toward the shop.

"Let's go," Manoling said. "We'll talk later."

He stopped to talk when they were about halfway back to Topside. Pushing the bike from the glaring road into the partial shade of an old coconut grove, he began abruptly, "Rafe thought she liked him, but she didn't."

"I believed her," Ronnie said. "I don't think she knows what happened to him."

"Then what is she afraid of? I wasn't going to hurt her. And she lied to me. She says she hasn't seen Rafe for weeks. But Rafe has gone to see her every weekend."

"Maybe he really went somewhere else."

"You mean Rafe is a liar? He isn't."

"Maybe something happened to make him change his mind. Of course I don't know Rafe," Ronnie said. "I wish I did. I wish I knew more about when he disappeared."

"That's what I'm going to tell you," Manoling said, but then he stopped, looking down at the ground and kicking at a small coconut that lay there.

"Don't you know how to begin?" Ronnie said. "It

doesn't matter. Start at the beginning or in the middle or at the end."

"I don't know the beginning or the end. It has to be the middle." But again he was silent.

"Then start at the beginning of the middle," Ronnie said at last. "Or tell me the theories."

"Theories?"

"There have to be some theories about what happened to him."

"Oh,—that!"

"Yes, that," Ronnie said. "What does your mother think? And your father? And the police—what did you call them?"

"The Constabulary."

"What's your theory? Do you have one?"

Still Manoling did not start to talk, but now Ronnie waited in silence, since asking questions had not hurried him.

He began at last, "My theory is that everybody else is wrong." He looked sharply at her. "Do you believe me?"

"Why not? If you say it's your theory, it's your theory."

"I mean, do you agree with me?"

"I suppose you have good reasons," Ronnie said. "But I don't know them yet. Why don't you tell me a little bit more?"

He said, "It's funny how hard it is to get started talking about him. I know him better than they do. Do you believe that?"

"I think if I had a brother or a sister," Ronnie said, "that I'd know him or her better than anyone else would. So I believe that."

"O.K. That's where we begin. I know—I *know*—"

"Don't get stuck again," she said. "Say it. Spit it out."

"I know he wouldn't do anything to make my mother worry. So I know he didn't disappear on purpose."

"Is that what was so hard for you to say?" Ronnie asked. "Forgive me if I faint with astonishment."

"You don't know how important it is. That's why you're laughing at me."

"O.K. I'll stop laughing, though really I wasn't laughing. I just never thought it was possible that he had disappeared on purpose. Why is that so important?"

"Because the Constabulary officers think he went off to join the Huks."

When she simply stared at him, he said, "That's what makes it so hard to tell!"

"You mean because there's so much that I don't know. Well, I'll be glad to learn. What are Huks?"

"You ought to have heard about them, Ronnie. They made a lot of trouble here. Everybody in our house can shoot a gun; I'm a good shot with a rifle and with a revolver. We had to keep a guard around the house day and night."

"Oh, you mean those people. But that was a long time ago. That's all over. They were all caught by—I can't think of his name."

"By Magsaysay. But they weren't all caught. A couple of their leaders have never been caught. They're still making trouble. And Rafe's room is full of maps of the islands and books about guerrillas and how they fight—and so that Constabulary captain that doesn't know Rafe at all says he's run off to join the Huks."

"Does anyone else believe that?" Ronnie asked. "Your mother? Your father? Charles?"

Manoling shook his head at each name.

"Then what are their theories? Come on, Manoling. Give! Don't make me pull the answers out of you."

"They think perhaps it was an accident. Perhaps he has been kidnapped. What else can they think?"

"Has there been a ransom note?"

"If he was kidnapped by Ilongots, they wouldn't ask for any ransom. Ilongots still take a head or two every year."

Again Ronnie stared at him, but this time it was not because she did not understand what he was talking about.

He said, "Yes. There are still Huks, and there are still headhunters. The savages of the present and the savages of the past. This is one kind of coexistence. You are older than I am, Ronnie, but in this country we have to learn some things fast. Some things you in your country haven't had to learn."

"Let's talk about Rafael," Ronnie said.

"We haven't stopped talking about him."

"Why do they think he might have been carried off by headhunters?"

"Because of the place this bike was found."

"But you don't think he ever went there. Isn't that what you told me?"

"Yes."

"And the bike hasn't a scratch on it. So how was there an accident?"

"You explain it," Manoling said.

"I couldn't explain anything," Ronnie said. "I'm all

mixed up. I feel as if I know less about Rafael all the time."

"Join the club," Manoling said. He held out his hand, she put hers in it, and they shook hands solemnly.

It was strange, Ronnie thought. The words and the handshake were corny, yet she felt indeed that she suddenly now belonged to an inner family circle held together by bewilderment and fear.

"Let's go," Manoling said, turning the motorbike toward the road. "I want to show you something before I tell you any more."

What he wanted to show her was on a low shelf in a dark corner of the garage. With her eyes dazzled by the noonday sun, she could hardly make out the small tank and the hoses attached to it, and the pair of flippers like the feet of a gigantic frog. Manoling said, "Rafael's scuba outfit."

"For skin diving. Yes, I see it."

"You see it plainly? It's here, isn't it?"

"Of course."

"And if it wasn't here, what would you see?"

"Well, what? A bare place on the shelf, I guess. There's another outfit, isn't there?"

"That's Charles's stuff," Manoling said. "Saturday morning there *was* a bare space beside it. I saw it. I say that Rafe had his scuba stuff with him. I say that he wasn't going to the Cagayan Valley. Nobody can do any skin diving there. I say he must have gone in some other direction. I say that somebody brought this stuff back. Because everyone knows it was here Sunday morning. And somebody took his bike up to the Cagayan Valley and left it there beside the road where the Constabulary found it. And somebody did that to confuse us about where Rafe had gone. Does that make sense or doesn't it?"

Ronnie said, "Of course it makes sense. Why——"

"Why? You wonder why I'm talking like this? It's because everyone else says the scuba stuff never left the garage at all. Rafe wasn't supposed to go skin diving without Charles. So they say that the outfit was here all the time and that in that dark corner I couldn't see it, or I'm remembering some other time, or it's all my imagination. Imagination? I *know!*"

Ronnie looked at him steadily. She was sure he believed what he was telling her.

"Do you believe me?" he asked. "Do you?"

"The corner is awfully dark, and Charles's stuff——" she began. C665139

"Charles's stuff! That's why *they* didn't notice anything. But *I saw*. I didn't tell anyone because I didn't want to get him into trouble for going without Charles." He was watching her carefully, waiting for her reaction. He added, "It never happened any other time. He never took it any other time except when Charles went, too."

She was satisfied. She believed him. But there was still a question to be answered. "Either you or Charles told me that the last time you saw Rafael was when he went off on the motorbike Saturday morning. Wouldn't some of this stuff show? Wouldn't it be on the back of the bike?"

"People don't say exactly what they mean. We saw him go downstairs. We were all at the table, finishing breakfast. Nobody really saw him leave. We just heard the bike."

"I understand," Ronnie said. "That makes sense."

"So now you'll help me?"

"Help you do what?"

"Help me find him, of course. Everybody else is looking for him in the wrong direction. Or else they think there's not much use—not much need to hurry— that he's——" He stopped, and Ronnie knew that he couldn't bear to finish that sentence.

She spoke quickly. "Then what's the right direction? And what are you going to do first? No, first was Celia, wasn't it? So what are you going to do next?"

"I don't know," he said. "But I do know I have a better chance of finding him than they have. And I'm never going to believe that he's joined the Huks. And I'm never going to give up, either. Never. I'm never going to—going to——"

Ronnie said it for him. "You're going to keep on believing that he's alive."

"That's right, Ronnie. That's *right.*"

Again they shook hands, and he squeezed her hand so hard that she almost cried out. But the tears that came to her eyes were because she felt what he was feeling about his brother. It was almost as if for the moment Rafael was her brother, too.

# ✳ 4 ✳

# Surprise Action

Ronnie and Manoling were slowly finishing their second dishes of coconut ice cream when someone came running up the stairs. "Charles," said Manoling, and Ronnie nodded. Heavy shoes and a light, quick step could mean no one else.

Charles halted beside the table. "What are you doing here?" he said to Manoling.

"Eating my lunch," Manoling said impertinently, but he said it with a grin and Charles smiled. Ronnie could see that they were good friends.

Charles said, "I didn't think that you could stay at school. I'm not surprised to see you here. What kind of ice cream is that?"

"Makapuno."

"Have you two eaten it all up?" Charles asked. He returned to the stairs and shouted to Engracia in Taga-

log. Then he came back and sat down at the table. "I've
been talking to the Constabulary."

"Any news of Rafe?" Manoling asked.

"Nothing at all."

"They're not looking," Manoling said. "They have
their theory. They're satisfied."

"It's not quite that simple, Manoling. Where are they
going to look? These mountains are worse than a hay-
stack and in them Rafe isn't as big as a needle. You know
how long Japs hid out in the mountains after the war."

"Are you saying it may be years before we find
Rafe?"

"I'm saying we have to face the facts."

There was a silence then, and Ronnie looked from
Charles to Manoling and back again, waiting for them
to continue.

It was Manoling who spoke first. "Is the Constabulary doing anything at all?"

"They've sent out requests for information, of
course. But what else can they do? They have a good
mountain troop, but where should they send them?"

"They're sitting back and waiting for news to come
in," Manoling said. He glanced at Ronnie. "That's what
I told you, isn't it?" She nodded, and he went on.
"They think he's joined the Huks. They think he could
come back if he wanted to. They think he could send
word. Isn't that true, Charles?"

"It's one theory they've offered."

"And it's crazy."

"I agree," Charles said. "It's crazy." To Engracia,
who at that moment put a large dish of ice cream in
front of him, he said, "*Salamat,* Engracia," and then
continued as he began to eat, "The question remains,

what can they do but hope for information to come in? You know that secrets can't be kept. If anyone knows anything, he's going to tell someone else. Sooner or later."

"You don't sound very hopeful," Manoling said.

"I'm simply facing the facts," Charles said. "And that is not giving up hope."

Nevertheless, Ronnie could feel hopelessness and gloom settling around them. She had been silent because she felt she had nothing to say, but now suddenly she felt that she must speak. She said, "It's like being a piece of fruit in a bowl and having jelly poured over you. If you let yourself get caught, before you know it, it will be too late."

Manoling and Charles both stared at her. "What are you talking about?" Manoling said.

She said, "You have to move fast before the jelly sets." Then when they still stared at her, she knew she had to explain. "I'm talking about giving up hope. You can't let yourself get caught."

"I see," Manoling said. "I thought you must be out of your mind."

"After all," Charles said, "we don't know you very well yet. 'Move fast before the jelly sets'? You mean that if we make up our minds that it's hopeless, it is hopeless. But didn't I say that I'm not giving up hope?"

"But I could feel hopelessness," Ronnie said. "In spite of what you said."

"And you thought we were going to get stuck in it. Well, it's a good warning. Though I can't think of any action to take except some action that hasn't anything to do with Rafe. I was going to ask you, Ronnie, if you wanted to fly over the mountains near the coast. Ron-

nie and I," he said to Manoling, "are interested in a
*kaiñgin* that I photographed up there. I want to locate
it. I'll tell you why later. Do you both want to go?
Have you had enough ice cream? Then let's go straight
to the hangar."

The single passenger's seat in the plane was easily
converted into a double seat by fastening a wide board
across it. An extra seat belt was already installed.

"It's comfortable enough for a short flight," Charles
said. "And safe, if you fasten the seat belts properly.
Help Ronnie, Manoling. It's a little complicated, Ronnie, but it works."

Ronnie was grateful for Manoling's help. Her fingers
were trembling. Flying in a big jet plane across the
Pacific hadn't seemed half as adventurous as this. She
tried to listen and understand as Charles and Manoling
checked off items on a written list, preparing for their
takeoff, but she could not keep her attention fixed on
anything. Looking at the nose of the plane, with its
bright orange stripes, she thought it was not very much
in front of her own nose; she felt as if she might fall
out. She gripped the board on which she sat and hoped
Manoling wouldn't guess that she was afraid.

Yet as soon as they were in the air, her fear was completely gone. Instead of seeing too much, she soon
wished she could see more. "A bird's-eye view," she
said aloud, though no one could hear her voice through
the noise of the plane. "This is really the way a bird
feels."

There were a few clouds scattered around them, and
beneath them was a wrinkled green velvet carpet that
she knew was jungle-covered mountains. Now and
then Manoling pointed to something and shouted a

few words, but she never heard enough to understand what he was saying.

Even if she had heard, she might not have understood, for her mind was lost in wonder. She knew only two directions, up, where she was, and down, down, down, where the earth was.

Then suddenly even her sense of up and down was gone, and everything everywhere was clouds and sky. Had they turned over? Were they flying upside down? She turned her eyes searching in all directions for a landmark.

There were no landmarks. There was no land. With a sigh, she found the explanation. They were over the ocean, and in the distance there was haze, with no horizon line showing where sky and water met.

The plane made a wide half-circle, and she saw ahead the long solid coast of the island. It was strangely thrilling to see. Knowing that no one could hear her, she cried, "Land, ho!"

Charles now guided the plane in a weaving pattern back and forth and back and forth over the mountains. Cloud shadows spotted the green carpet with moving patches of darkness. Charles touched her and spoke, pointing downward, and she knew that she was to watch for that strip she had seen in his pictures. Obediently she tried to discipline her eyes and make them look with purpose.

But the clouds were swelling in number and size, until the plane was flying into white blindness too often for them to make a useful search. While they were inside a single cloud they could easily pass over the place they hunted for, and never know it. Charles waved a hand and shouted something.

A short time later they taxied along his airstrip and stopped in front of his hangar.

"What was that all about?" Manoling asked as soon as he could be heard. "A kaiñgin! Who cares about a kaiñgin? There's nothing worth looking for in those mountains anyhow."

"What about orchids?" Charles asked. "What about Negritos? What about valuable Philippine hardwood, like narra, tindalo, camagon, or molave, the Queen of Woods. I've made a little study of molave."

"I know," Manoling said. "I've heard your little lecture about it. It's as hard as your heart. Keeping secrets from me. That trip was wasted."

"Not wasted!" Ronnie said. "I never felt before that I was really flying. I didn't feel that I was really here, in the islands, until just now."

"We'll go up again the next chance we get," Charles said. "And you'll see, Ronnie, that Manoling will want to come. Now, let's get the plane inside the hangar and go home and see if there's any news."

But there was no news. There was only the family, as usual, trying to hide the worries they all felt.

"Ronnie must sit at my right," said Doña Paz at dinner that night. "So that we can become better acquainted. We have had no chance. Charles, you sit at Ronnie's other side. And Manoling will sit in his place at my left, although he is a bad boy for leaving school and should sit in a corner with his face to the wall. But I love him too much to make him do it."

"He's spoiled," his father said, but he said it with affection. "Children in this country are always spoiled. But it seems to be good for them. We'll spoil you, too, Ronnie. I hope you don't mind."

Ronnie said, "I think I'll like it."

Her Uncle Frank was kind, but he seemed to her very tired. She had already put that in a half-finished letter to her mother, and now she decided that she ought to underline the words. Perhaps it was Rafael's disappearance that made him look as he did; she couldn't know. Of course she did know that he had been in Santo Tomás as a prisoner of the Japanese all through the war, and that had aged him. And he ran a big sugar mill.

As for Doña Paz, what should she write about her in the letter? Beside her, Ronnie felt large and clumsy. They were about the same height, but in high heels and standing very erect, holding her head very proudly, and wearing the Philippine dress with the great transparent sleeves, Doña Paz was like—what? A royal butterfly?

She and old Engracia and Teresita and Celia were the only Filipinos that Ronnie had met. They were as different from each other as from Ronnie herself. Doña Paz was beautiful, and in spite of being tiny, she was somehow awesome. Although Ronnie's mother had been telling Ronnie all her life about Pacita, Ronnie found her a mystery.

"Where were you all day, Doña Paz?" Charles asked.

"Where I always am on Wednesday. At the Mother and Baby Clinic." She turned to Ronnie. "I'll take you one day soon. Then, if you like it, I'll take you often. We need help. Do you like babies?"

"I don't know," Ronnie said. "I don't think I've ever seen any up close."

"But you do know what they're like?" Manoling asked.

Ronnie nodded, smiling. "I've heard a little about them."

"Then it's time you learned at firsthand," Doña Paz said. "And it's good to be busy." An expression so desolate came over her face that tears filled Ronnie's eyes. But the expression vanished quickly, and Ronnie was winking back the tears long seconds after Doña Paz's mask was once more in place.

"What did you do alone all day, Ronnie?" Frank asked.

"But I wasn't alone," she answered. "Manoling was here and then Charles."

"Company enough for any girl," Doña Paz said, "or perhaps too much?"

"Oh, never too much!" Ronnie cried, and everyone laughed.

"I'm afraid they are like babies to you," Doña Paz said.

"Babies!" said Ronnie, feeling her eyes grow wide with surprise.

Her Uncle Frank explained, "She means that you've never seen them up close before." He added, "You're very much like your mother when she was your age, Ronnie."

"I am?" This was another surprise. "Do you think I'll be like her when I'm more grown up?"

"Do you want to be?" Charles asked. "Is she perfect?"

"Nobody's perfect, I guess," Ronnie said. "She doesn't think she's perfect. I know I'll never be perfect. But she can be wonderful when she wants to be. Everybody thinks so, not just me."

"A very good answer, and that puts you in your

place, Charles," said Doña Paz. "You are a younger
brother. You had a worm's-eye view. I remember all
that. You used to quarrel; oh, how you used to quarrel!
But to all the rest of the world you presented a united
front."

"Whatever that is," Charles said. "Like Siamese
twins?"

"Like England and the United States," Manoling
said. "Like the Philippines and the United States."

"You should be at school, learning more about all
that," his mother said.

"My schoolwork is O.K."

She said, "O.K. is not good enough. But we will talk
of that later. Now we must not argue. We must enjoy
this good food. We will lose the best cook we ever had
if he doesn't feel appreciated."

But she herself, Ronnie noticed, ate very little. It
was as if the food choked her. She would lift her fork
toward her mouth and then put it down again, sometimes to sit looking down at her plate, with her face
expressionless, occasionally to talk.

Her voice was bright and quick, and her words were
distinct, as if each was neatly clipped off as it was
spoken. Perhaps she was more like a hummingbird
than a butterfly, Ronnie thought. Yet neither of those
creatures had the strength that she could feel in Doña
Paz.

Ronnie was hungry and she ate well. So did Manoling and so did her two uncles. She noticed that. She
noticed everything. She had heard about these people
all her life. She had seen pictures of them. All had
been described to her over and over again. Yet everything about them was new and unexpected. Of course

she was seeing them at a time when they were all under a strain, but that was not what made the difference. The difference was between what she had imagined and what was real.

Somehow she had believed that what was imagined would always be more surprising than what was real, like fairy tales and science fiction compared to life in boarding school. But she had been wrong. What was real, what was human, was more surprising.

She did not listen much to their words. They talked mostly of things she knew little or nothing about: the last presidential election and the political murders that were part of it, coffee growing, the rice harvest of the local farmers, the advantages and the disadvantages of the national dress called *barong Tagalog*, the repair of the roads in the provinces, the weather, a new dam on some big river, an earthquake of the week before, and a dozen other things.

What Ronnie was listening to was underneath the words. It was a feeling that she described to herself in words that Doña Paz had already used. A united front. They presented a united front to all the rest of the world.

Not Siamese twins but Siamese quadruplets, she thought. Then she thought of the missing Rafael, who would make the quadruplets into quintuplets, and she felt a great loneliness for him and for the family, and also for herself. For she had forgotten him for an instant, and that reminded her of something else she had forgotten. She was an outsider. Forgetting Rafael was both reminder and proof.

Doña Paz returned to the subject of Manoling's

schoolwork. "O.K. is not good enough, Manoling," she said again. "How about your Latin?"

"A week away from school," Manoling said, "won't make things much worse."

"A week," his mother repeated, and there was a silence. Ronnie knew what all were thinking, and this time she was united with them. Was Rafael going to be found in a week?

But she was thinking of something more. She asked, "What Latin?"

"Didn't you ever hear of Latin?" Manoling said. "It's a dead language that should be left to rest in peace."

"I mean, what year of Latin?"

"It feels like the thousandth. And it may be, before I get any sense out of Caesar's wars."

Caesar? That was wonderful luck.

Ronnie took a deep breath to quiet her excitement. She said, "I've had that. I think Latin's easy. I could help you."

Doña Paz said, "Then waste no time. Begin tonight."

It sounded as if she had smiled while she spoke, but Ronnie did not see. She was looking down at her plate, trying to conceal her delight from Manoling, who would not be pleased.

They had all been careful not to make her feel that a house guest at such a time was not welcome. Yet it was a wonderful relief to her to have something useful to do, something that only she could do.

If she could do it. She glanced sideways at Manoling.

No. He was not pleased. He was not at all pleased.

## ❀ 5 ❀

# *Ground*
# *Observation*

Ronnie and Manoling on the motorbike left behind them the barrio where Celia's father had his shop. Now the road was new to Ronnie. It would soon, Manoling had told her, arrive at a main road, and they would turn east there, toward the mountains.

The cook had made a picnic lunch for them and Engracia had brought it, along with a raincoat for Ronnie, scolding Manoling all the time in Tagalog.

"She says I'm crazy to go on a picnic today," Manoling told Ronnie. "But she doesn't know how crazy I really am."

They had stopped at the church and Manoling had prayed again, this time with Ronnie kneeling beside him on the stone floor. She had never knelt in a church before, nor dreamed of going into an empty church to pray, but this morning it seemed a natural and important thing for her to do. She knew what Manoling prayed for, and she too prayed for help in finding Rafael.

While they were in the barrio it had been raining, but now the sun shone again between clouds and was reflected with blinding brilliance by the water in the rice paddies.

And then sunshine and paddies were both gone, and Ronnie and Manoling on the motorbike were in the mountains, under a gray sky, slowly climbing.

Ronnie knew Florida well and she had believed that therefore she knew all about the tropics. But she was discovering that Florida was hardly more than a sample. It was as if she had seen a leaf and had believed it was a tree. Now she was seeing the tree.

In fact, she was seeing thousands of trees. The mountain forest awed her. She could sometimes see the road far ahead, or at least the break in the forest showing where the road must be, and she had to admire the roadbuilders. The conquest of the forest seemed to her more marvelous than the conquest of the mountains.

"The mountains are quiet. They're just standing here," she said to Manoling when they stopped to drink from a small waterfall beside the road. "But the trees and all the vines are alive. They want to grow over the road and take it back into the jungle. I feel as if the jungle is reaching out for me, too. It scares me."

Manoling looked scornfully at her. "You're mixed in your facts," he said. "Trees are trees and vines are vines. They don't reach out for you. They're alive but they can't do anything but grow bigger. And don't think the mountains stand still. We have earthquakes.

If you want to be afraid, that's something to be afraid of. When the mountains reach out for you."

"You could get lost in this jungle and never get out again."

"Not if you kept your head," Manoling said. "You can be your own enemy in the jungle. But the jungle isn't an enemy any more than it's a friend." He stamped his feet. "Are you tired?"

"Well—it's good to stop for a minute. And this water is wonderful." She bent her head to catch a direct mouthful and drew back shaking her wet hair. "I guess it's better to make a cup with my hands. Do any people live in these mountains?"

"Maybe a few Negritos."

"Are they headhunters?"

He laughed. "Do you feel them reaching out for you? No. They don't take heads. They shoot poisoned arrows."

Ronnie looked around uneasily.

"Don't worry. They won't shoot at us. They shoot to get food and they're not cannibals. These aren't the Cannibal Islands, you know."

"You needn't make fun of me," Ronnie said. "Just because I'm a stranger."

"O.K.," he said. "But you ought not to be such a stranger. Your mother is American but she was born here. You ought to know more about us. Negritos—this is a quick lecture while we stretch—are tiny, very black, with frizzy hair. They were probably the first inhabitants. Then Malays came—that's what I am, part Malay—and the Malays drove the Negritos into the mountains. Then the Chinese came, and then the English, and then the Dutch—did I leave out the Spanish? They came before the English and they stayed longer. Then the Americans came. And then the Japanese. The end. I hope. Let's go, shall we? Climb on and hang on."

Traffic on the mountain road was light. It was chiefly of trucks, small and large, and there was a bus going in the opposite direction. They overtook two or three trucks going in their own direction, but nothing overtook them, even when they stopped to eat a sandwich.

It was nearly noon then and they were in sight of the ocean, about to descend from the mountains into the Baler River valley. It wasn't long after that stop before they rode into the town of Baler, passed through it, and arrived at Port Aurora, on Baler Bay. The sun had come out again and everything in the town and at the port was hot and sleepy.

They got off the bike here and walked along, pushing it.

Ronnie saw a small steamer at a wharf, with no movement anywhere about it. A number of small motorboats were anchored or tied to buoys a short distance from the shore, two or three of them pleasure boats, perhaps, but most of them, Manoling said, fishing boats. "To catch fish to make a living, not for fun." Pulled up on the muddy beach were dugout boats that he called *bancas*. Two men, far away, seemed to Ronnie to be dancing in a slow ballet. Manoling said, "They're examining a big net and folding it." No other persons were in sight.

Ronnie yawned. She felt suddenly too sleepy to know or care where she was going.

"Here," Manoling said, reaching across the bike to

catch her arm. "You're stumbling. If I can find a dry place——"

No place was dry, for it had rained and the ground anyhow was low and marshy, but he seated Ronnie on the raincoat, beside a small closed shack, with the bike against the wall beside her. "Stay here," he said, "while I talk to those fishermen."

With her knees bent up, her arms on them and her head on her arms, she sat, half-dozing, half-dreaming. A Rafael who was much like Manoling came and went in her mind. Baler was the place where he had come for skin diving. There were flippers on his feet. Now he was swimming. He swam in and out the windows and doors of a castle made of coral rock, and goldfish swam in and out, meeting him, weaving past him, fins fluttering. The goldfish were as big as he was or he was as small as the goldfish, and around the castle the seaweed grew like a jungle, thicker and thicker, reaching out for him as he passed——

She opened her eyes and raised her head. Manoling was there. He said, "Nobody saw him Saturday. They all know him here."

"And they'd tell you the truth?"

"You mean they might have helped him disappear? Or they might be covering up an accident? No. I know. Don't ask me how I know, but I do." He turned the bike around for their trip back.

"Listen a minute, Manoling, before we start. Rafael wasn't supposed to go diving without Charles. That's one reason why they won't believe you when you say the flippers and things were gone. And you say he's honorable, and wouldn't sneak to do anything. Or at least you say he's not a liar, and sneaking is a sort of lie.

So why did you come here to find out if he went diving?"

"I don't know what he did or why he did it," Manoling said. "If I knew that I'd know where he is now. But he did take his scuba outfit, and so I think he was coming here, and so I'm trying to find out if he got here and if anybody knows what he did here. So stop trying to confuse me and get on the bike. I'm going to ask about him in the town."

But in Baler, too, no one that Manoling talked to had seen his brother or the motorbike on Saturday.

Traffic on their return trip through the mountains was heavier than it had been in the morning. They passed about a dozen trucks and cars going in their direction. Then, when they stopped to finish their sandwiches, they saw the same trucks and cars pass them. And then, back on the bike, they soon overtook and passed the others once more. By this time they seemed like old friends, and some of the drivers waved at Ronnie.

One small closed truck, but briefly, seemed like an enemy. They overtook it quite soon for the second time, because it had halted at the edge of the road, and one man had his head over the engine while another leaned against the side, watching the oncoming traffic. Ronnie, as they passed, saw him turn to watch them while one hand jerked to his hip as if reaching for a gun.

But of course the hand stayed there, the movement was meaningless or at least unimportant, there was no gun, and the whole idea was ridiculous. Nevertheless, she tried to remember the name on the side of the truck. TINY something-or-other, she thought it was, but was mistaken about that, too, as she learned when the truck passed them again. They had stopped to stretch their cramped legs. TINAPAYAN SAMPA-GUITA, the name read. Manoling said that it meant Sampaguita Bakery, the *sampaguita* being the national flower of the Philippines, a small white jasmine.

"More words for my vocabulary," Ronnie said. "And that's enough for today."

It was nearly dark before they reached Topside, and when they were inside the house, where the lights were turned on, it seemed to be night indeed. They had walked the motorbike up the hill, and their rubber-soled shoes were quiet on the stairs. Their arrival in the sala took Doña Paz and Manoling's father and Charles by surprise. Ronnie could feel the tension relax as she and Manoling appeared.

Not a word of reproach was spoken, yet she was ashamed of adding to the anxiety in which this family was living. She glanced at Manoling and guessed that he, too, was feeling guilty. They had left a note saying they might be late. They had tried to avoid causing worry. But everyone in this house existed now in a state of suspense, and the smallest thing could make them tremble.

Manoling asked, "Any news?" But he must have known, as Ronnie did, merely from one quick look at the faces turned to them, that there had been no news.

After dinner Ronnie continued with her new job of helping Manoling with his Latin.

They were making a bad beginning. "This Caesar," Manoling said, throwing the book on the table, "has been dead a thousand years."

Ronnie didn't answer him at once. She moved her

chair nearer to his, sat down, and reached for his book. She longed to succeed in this job. She had a picture of everyone's astonishment if Manoling suddenly progressed ahead of his class. But she knew the picture was not realistic. It would be success enough if she could get him interested.

She said, "Manoling! A thousand years? No. You're wrong. He's been dead two thousand years. He's twice as dead as you thought he was." She opened the book to the table of contents and found the page number she wanted. "Here." She turned to the page. "Read it for yourself. Your book is like the one I used, except that mine stays open better. I've used it longer."

He was still not sitting down, but he glanced at the page and said, "Forty-four B.C. More than two thousand. So, twice as dead, and who cares?"

"I guess nobody cares. I guess nobody would want him alive today."

"Nobody wanted him alive then," Manoling said. "He got killed, didn't he? By people he thought were friends?"

She didn't say anything.

"Aren't you going to tell me about Lincoln and Kennedy? They got killed, too. Aren't you going to say that he was a great man or people wouldn't remember him for two thousand years?"

"Why should I tell you things that you know?" Ronnie said. "And I don't know much you don't know about him except how to read this book. I should think you'd like it better than I do."

"Why?"

"You know why, Manoling. Because it's about war.

Because he was a great general. Great generals today know all about Caesar's wars."

"They'd be better generals," Manoling said, "if they knew all about guerrilla wars. This Caesar," he pulled out his chair and sat down, "I bet he didn't know half as much about guerrilla fighting as my brother Rafe does." He leaned closer and spoke under his breath. "You heard what I said? 'Does.' My father tonight said something about what Rafe always *did*."

Ronnie nodded. She had noticed that, too.

"And we asked them if there was any news, but they didn't ask us. And we were the only ones that did anything today about looking for him."

Ronnie nodded again.

But all this was leading farther each moment from a Latin lesson. She said, "How do you know that Caesar didn't know anything about guerrilla fighting? Have you read enough to be sure? I've read it all, but I don't know, because I don't know anything about guerrillas."

"You ought to know," Manoling said. "Rafe says everyone ought to know. And since Rafe isn't here right now, I'll have to tell you myself. Do you know that it takes up to fifty regular soldiers to fight one guerrilla? That's because guerrillas don't stand and fight. They hit, and then they run and hide. And hiding—that means a hundred different things. They melt into the background . . ."

Every word took them farther and farther from a Latin lesson. Ronnie took a pencil and a pad of paper. She said, "I'm going to make notes. And then we can compare them with things that Caesar does."

And that was the last time that evening that Caesar's

name was mentioned. From talking of guerrillas, Manoling went on to talk of Rafe and to the question of what to do next in trying to trace him. He did not find any answer.

# 6

# Aerial Observation

Again Ronnie and Manoling were flying with Charles toward the ocean. This afternoon, too, there were clouds, but they were smaller and fewer. Charles had said he did not think they would increase. They were above the plane, woolly white sheep in a vast blue field, and now and then their shadows darkened the green jungle below.

The plane reached the ocean, turned a quarter circle, and flew south. Then Charles turned it west, and began a course of weaving like a shuttle, back and forth from east to west and from west to east, progressing gradually northward.

In this way Charles intended to cover all the area where his pictures of the airstrip might have been taken. With the three of them watching, he hoped that the break in the mountain forest would be seen.

Manoling hadn't seen the pictures and didn't know yet why Charles wanted to find this mysterious kaiñgin.

Suddenly Ronnie's eager eyes glimpsed a yellowish-greenish patch that appeared and disappeared as the plane was turning. Could this be it? Didn't this have to be it? The questions were hardly formed in her mind, but she was already shouting and pointing. The shout was unheard in the noise of the plane, but the pointing was signal enough.

But neither Charles nor Manoling noticed her pointing finger, for they were pointing, too. The three of them must all have seen it at the same time. The plane was already tilting to circle back and give them a better look.

It was without doubt the same straight-edged patch shown in the pictures. There was the river, snaking through the bottom of the valley, and halfway up the mountain on a sort of shelf was the place they'd been searching for. At the moment of their return, sunlight between two cloud shadows spotlighted it for them dramatically.

The next part of Charles's plan was to find a landmark to guide him if he should come again. He made another circle. Now he would fly the plane straight to the east, across the shoreline and out over the ocean, and then turn back toward land. They were all to look for some unusual formation, either of the shore or of the profile of the mountains or, better yet, of both.

The ocean was in sight; it was near; now it was very near; now the water's edge was below them; now they were past it.

The coast was rugged, with no beach and with cliffs

that Ronnie guessed were much taller and steeper than
they looked from the plane. There were small islands,
some merely bare rocks, but some green with plants or
bushes or perhaps with trees. There was one group of
these like a lucky four-leaf clover, and she shouted
and pointed down.

As before, Charles and Manoling were shouting and
pointing, too. And already the clover was behind them.

Now for the skyline. Charles flew far enough so that
they would have a good, long, distant view. Then he
turned.

Ronnie shook her head. The mountains were like a
parade of dark green elephants with parades of dark
blue elephants and then light blue elephants behind
it, and probably the same parades went for miles and
miles along the coast in both directions.

But perhaps the clover-leaf islands were enough.
Charles pointed at them again as the plane passed
over.

They spiraled down over the greenish-yellowish
patch for a nearer look.

It appeared empty. Ronnie could see nothing human
and nothing man-made down there. There was no
sparkle of light on the projecting nose of a hidden
plane. There was nothing, she thought, but the wind
that blows and the grass that grows green.

The plane spiraled up again, and a sudden feeling
made Ronnie look at Charles. He was staring at her
and at Manoling with a curious expression on his face.
He seemed to be asking a question, and she guessed at
it, and nodded. Landing down there had not been part
of the plan, but she was not surprised at what happened next.

The ground was rough. They bumped and jounced. Charles taxied the plane to the south end of the patch and turned it, its tail toward the jungle, ready to take off.

The silence was strange and Charles's voice was loud. He said, "I hated to waste the chance to look the place over. I don't think I've got you kids into anything dangerous."

Manoling said, "If you can get down, you can get up, can't you?" Then he added, "It's like an airstrip. But what's an airstrip doing here?"

"That's the question," Charles said. "So let's explore. Help me block the wheels, Manoling, and then we'll see that side first." He pointed to the place where he and Ronnie thought a plane had been hidden.

The sun was very hot and the grass was hard to walk on, for there was a stubble of old brown grass beneath the tough green blades. They crossed toward the long east side of the strip.

The jungle was like a wall. Thorny green vines laced the trees together. Where Ronnie could see through a vine, it was only to see more vines beyond it. She was sure that no one could pass through this wall without first cutting an opening.

But it was projecting from this wall that the nose of a plane had appeared in the pictures. If it was the nose of a plane. Until they were more than halfway down the strip, she felt that she and Charles must have been mistaken.

Then they came to the break. Perhaps Charles had seen it as they landed, but she had not. It was like a wide door over which hung a few vines, enough to make the opening seem a part of the wall unless you were looking straight at it.

Charles went cautiously ahead here, but in a moment gave them a sign to follow.

It was like entering a green cave. The light was dim, and the cave was cool. Ronnie shivered a little.

For a few seconds they stood quietly staring around. Gradually Ronnie could see details, the leafy ceiling, the surprising depth of the cave. Then Manoling took a couple of steps away from the others, looking at the ground and then stopping, pointing with his toe. He said, "That place out there looks like an airstrip, and this place right here looks as if a heavy wheel had stood here." He turned his head and pointed again, this time with a finger. "And another wheel stood right there. Someone has kept an airplane here."

"We agree," Charles said. "Don't we, Ronnie?"

"*Yes!*" she said, too excited to say more.

"Who?" Manoling asked. "Why? What do you and Ronnie know about it? Who told you?"

"There are plenty of questions," Charles said, "and the only one I can answer is how I found it. I found it by accident. In a picture I took. Well, let's see all we can see."

Starting at the near wall, he began pacing off the width of the opening from the strip. Manoling, seeing this, stepped off the distance between the hollows where the wheels had stood, and then began searching for a third wheel mark.

Ronnie knew it was silly for her to think of imitating them. She began to prowl slowly along the wall of the cave.

This wall was not so forbidding as the outside wall.

There were fewer vines and she could see through them easily into the army of tree trunks beyond. The trunks were very tall, not branching out until they were many feet above her head, and some of them were giants, the mightiest tree trunks she had ever seen.

The ground now under her feet was soft and springy, for she was walking on a thick layer of decaying leaves.

She was looking for nothing in particular, and she did not expect to find anything of importance. She felt that they had already made the one important discovery when they found the opening in the jungle wall and the wheel marks of the plane. But her eyes were open and she was using them.

What she noticed could hardly have been called a path. It was only an opening in the cave wall through which it would be easy to move by pushing aside a loose vine. She pushed the vine aside and took a couple of steps among the trees.

Now she saw a wide but not tall heap of something only a few steps farther. Vines covered it, but they did not conceal a green canvas covering beneath them. She lifted an edge of the canvas and looked underneath. The heap was made of big square gasoline tins, placed on a low bamboo platform that kept them just above the ground. She moved one a little and learned that it was full.

She was sure that Charles or Manoling would have made this discovery if they had come this way first, but she was pleased to have made it herself.

She stepped back through the opening and called them.

Charles counted the tins, trying each one to find if

it was full, looking for labels but finding none. "Good going, Ronnie," he said. "This doesn't tell us anything we don't know already, but it reinforces it."

"But they've been here a long time," she said. "They're rusty."

"Not very rusty considering this climate. And I don't think they've been here long. It's always damp in the jungle, you know. The trees always drip, whether it's raining or not. This is good. And now let's see what more there is."

They did not find much more. There was a pile of empty food tins, almost completely grown over, crumbling with rust. At the back of the cave there was a path that led to the rising mountainside, where they found a cataract of cold, delicious water that joined a stream running south into the jungle. And that was all.

After landing the plane on his own airstrip and locking it in the hangar, Charles took Ronnie and Manoling to Topside and then drove away. When he returned, the family had almost finished their dinner.

He had found the answer to one of their questions. "The Constabulary know all about that strip," he told them. "Or so they tell me. It was cleared during the war by our guerrillas. They thought American planes might need a place to land in that area."

"But you landed there easily today," Frank Richardson said. "Manoling has been telling us about it. No strip would stay clear so long unless it was kept clear."

"I told them that. I told them I'm sure a plane was there only a few days ago. They said they'd look into the matter."

"Who do they think might be using it?" Frank Richardson asked.

"They didn't make any suggestions. In fact, I don't think I convinced them that the place is being used."

"What do you think yourself, Charles?"

Manoling answered quickly, "Huks."

The two men nodded. "Perhaps," Charles said.

"They are still full of life and venom," his brother said.

"But," Charles added, "I don't think the Huks ever had any planes."

"No reason they never will have any," his brother said. "And if it's not Huks, who is it?"

When no one else answered at once, Ronnie spoke. "Somebody who shouldn't be using it."

Charles and Frank and Manoling all laughed at this, and Charles said, "I couldn't have said it better myself."

Doña Paz's reaction was different. She had been listening without a comment. Now she said, "I can see you are all excited about this adventure. What would you call it? A divine experience? A gas? A blast? Or some other absurdity? Please do not repeat it, Charles. I do not like the thought of you flying into danger, but you are a man, you must do as you choose. But please do not take Ronnie and Manoling again."

"I was sure the place was deserted today," Charles said. "Otherwise I wouldn't have landed."

"But someone might have come after you landed."

"No one did, Pacita."

"You are usually lucky, Charles, but nevertheless, if you please——? You understand me."

"I understand you, Pacita."

"I notice that you are not apologizing or making

promises," she said. "But if you understand me, that is enough, I hope."

He repeated, "I understand you, Pacita."

Ronnie thought he took his scolding well, and she, too, could understand Doña Paz. But she felt rebellious. She had feared no danger that afternoon on that lonely mountainside. It was so far away and so empty and so quiet and so peaceful that she had felt safe every moment while she was there.

But of course Doña Paz was thinking about Rafael, and of course everything worried her now. Ronnie could feel her anxiety.

"No news of your brother?" she asked Manoling as soon as they had been left alone in the dining room for Manoling's Latin lesson.

"I didn't ask. If there was news, we'd hear it. They didn't even mention his name tonight. Did you notice?"

She had noticed. "But they were all thinking about him."

"Yes. It's the only thing there is to think about. It's the only thing that seems real. That place up in the mountains—that's more important, probably. More important to more people. Rafe is only one family's trouble. That place——" He stared at his open book, but he was not seeing it. "It doesn't seem important. It doesn't seem real. Only one thing is real: Rafael is gone. But I can't believe that. I keep thinking he's going to walk in any minute. I look up at the door—but he isn't there."

Ronnie could think of nothing to say.

"And nobody does anything," Manoling went on. "And what we did yesterday—that didn't help. And today was wasted."

"But we did something Charles reported to the Constabulary. Right away. You can't say today was wasted."

"Sure. I said it was probably important. But not to me."

"But it was good to think of something else for a while," Ronnie said. "Wasn't it?"

"No. And I suppose now you think it would be good to think of Caesar for a while. That's what you were leading up to."

Ronnie shook her head. "I was wondering about doing something else before we start on Caesar."

"Anything is better than starting on Caesar," said Manoling. He closed the book with a bang. "What do you want to do?"

"I lost a gold pin that I was wearing this afternoon. It isn't very valuable, I guess, but my father gave it to me. I thought it might be in the plane. Could we——"

He interrupted her. "Go and look? Sure."

"It isn't too late to go tonight?"

"No. Better go tonight. Sometimes Charles leaves early in the morning. He goes up to his coffee plantation in the Cagayan Valley, or he goes to Manila, and sometimes he's gone for a week. I'll tell my mother what we're going to do and get the key to the hangar and a couple of flashlights."

They didn't find the pin, but they found something else. In the bucket seat under the board on which Ronnie and Manoling had sat, Ronnie found a watch-bracelet. She held it out to Manoling. "This must be yours or Charles's."

"I didn't lose mine, and he would have——" He stopped speaking as he turned the flashlight on the watch, and Ronnie could see his hands begin to shake.

"What's wrong, Manoling? What's the matter?"

He said, "This is——" and then he paused, lifting the watch to his ear. "It's running!"

"So what?"

"It's running!" he said again, and his voice squeaked. "Come on, we have to get back to the house. This is Rafael's watch. Ronnie! Are you listening? This is— come on! Let's go!"

"It means he's alive," said Doña Paz, putting the watch to her ear. "I will not hear you if you say anything different."

No one said anything different, but other opinions were possible. The watch was Rafael's watch, and it was running, but that was all they could be certain of. It proved nothing else and it asked more questions than it could answer.

Who had put it in the plane? And when? And why?

Was it the beginning of a demand for ransom?

If it was already in the plane when they fastened the board over the seat, why hadn't they noticed it?

Had there been a chance that afternoon for anyone to slip into the hangar?

Had someone broken into the hangar earlier that evening?

"I think that's when it was done," Charles said. "The padlock on the door is rusty. It doesn't always lock. I must have been careless. The only sure thing," he added, "is that nobody put that watch in the plane while it stood on the side of that mountain. We were alone up there. Miles away from every other human being in the world."

# ❋ 7 ❋

# *Obstacle: Weather*

The watch had been found on Friday. On Saturday the Weather Bureau in Manila sent out warnings of an approaching typhoon.

Ronnie had seen hurricanes when she lived in Florida. Wind and water had sometimes severely damaged her father's avocado and lime groves, and she knew that her mother feared these storms, but she herself had secretly enjoyed them. It had been fun to have the electric power fail, and to sit up all night using flashlights and oil lamps and listening to a battery radio for news of the storm's approach.

Since typhoons were like hurricanes, but larger because they were born and grew strong over a larger ocean, she expected a typhoon to be more fun than a hurricane.

It was not.

One reason, Ronnie knew, was that she was older. Warnings of danger now sounded like warnings of danger.

Another reason was that to her the house seemed terribly open and flimsy. Manoling told her it had stood through many years of storms, some of them very strong. He told her that it would stand through this one. "The easier it is for water to come in," he said, "the easier it is to sweep it out."

A third reason was that the storm was indeed larger and more furious than anything she remembered, although only an edge of it passed over Topside.

And yet another reason was that the storm had stopped everything else. For a while it forced them to be slaves to all its whims and orders.

On Saturday when the weather report on the radio told them that typhoon signal two was up at Manila, Ronnie went with Doña Paz to the Baby Clinic and weighed babies and helped with charts until noon. Then signal four went up and they returned to Topside. They did not leave Topside again until the storm had passed.

Manoling's father stayed there with them. There was a responsible man at the sugar mill. But Charles did not stay. Typhoon signal two indicated a storm passing to the north of Manila; signal four indicated that the typhoon was a dangerous one. As Topside was a hundred and fifty kilometers north of Manila, it would probably get stronger winds than the city would. Without waiting for further signals, Charles flew his plane south, for he had little faith in the strength of his hangar. He had business in Manila anyway. And if necessary he would fly on to Panay or Cebu.

Ronnie was bored. The hours dragged. Everything was uncomfortable. Her clothes were clammy. The soles of her shoes grew little forests of mold. The cushions on the chairs and the pillow and mattress on her bed all smelled strongly of the kapok that stuffed them. The air was chilly, but a sweater felt too warm.

Manoling was bored, too. In their joint boredom, he learned more about Caesar than he had expected to learn, and she learned a surprising number of facts about guerrilla warfare.

Along with the tension caused by the storm she felt an increase in the tension about Rafael. Doña Paz was very silent, but Ronnie could hear the silence screaming, "Where is Rafael during this storm? Is the rain falling on him? Can he feel it? Can he *feel* it?" She knew that it was terrible for Doña Paz to believe that he was suffering during this typhoon, but that it was worse for her to think of him lying somewhere in the rain but beyond all feeling.

Sometimes Doña Paz talked a little quietly with her husband. But he usually had little to say. He walked aimlessly around the house or he walked back and forth on the side of the verandah that was comparatively dry, or he read a little, or he sat thinking.

The rain came first in sudden downpours, and then in fierce squalls. Sometimes the wind howled and sometimes it shrieked. Sometimes, with two voices, it howled and shrieked at the same time. Sometimes there was an undertone of moaning that filled Ronnie's heart with sadness and terror.

But meanwhile Caesar fought the powerful Veneti and conquered them.

And Ronnie was drilled on the principles that guerrillas got their strength from the people, that they fought in a different way from regular soldiers but not without their own rules and their own kind of organization, that you had to understand them as the first step to fighting them, and that you could never succeed against them until you had won the people away from them.

It was good luck, she thought, more than good sense that made her see that the Veneti were, in a way, guerrillas, and that in fighting them Caesar began by using Manoling's principle of understanding them. For a short time Ronnie and Manoling were both interested in working on this idea.

Yet the storm had a way of seizing and holding everyone's attention. Everything else took second place.

Ronnie began to come alive again, she began to think again, when at last, Monday afternoon, it was plain that winds and rain were diminishing. But her thoughts had turned into new directions, as if they'd been caught up in a squall and tossed about.

Charles had said that he was sure of one thing: that Rafael's watch had not been put in the plane while it stood on that mountain airstrip. Now Ronnie began asking herself, Why not?

"Why not?" she asked Manoling. "Maybe somebody was there."

"Who? Rafe? But he didn't let us see him? That's a nutty idea."

Nutty or not, it stayed in her mind.

And that evening another idea kept coming between her and Caesar's battles. "Listen, Manoling," she said.

"Why don't you make a list of everything you know about Rafael's disappearance?"

"I don't need a list. I know what I know."

"Then I'll make a list," she said. "And you can tell me if it's right."

She made a list slowly, and then copied it, putting it in better order. On paper it was disappointing, but she read it to Manoling anyhow.

"One. Rafael had some plan in his mind when he went away that day, but he didn't tell anyone what it was.

"Two. He went on his motorbike and took his diving stuff.

"Three. This was against the rules. It was not like Rafael to go against the rules.

"Four. Nobody knows where he went.

"Five. The motorbike was found—where, Manoling? I had to leave a blank."

"In the Cagayan Valley, right beside the highway, eighty kilometers north of here," Manoling said. "I don't know what good this will do. But go on."

"Six. The bike was O.K. It hadn't been in an accident.

"Seven. The diving stuff came back here. It was O.K., too, wasn't it?"

"Yes," Manoling said. "I checked it."

"Eight. Rafael's girl, Celia, was afraid to talk to you.

"Nine. Rafael hadn't been diving in Baler.

"Ten. Someone put his watch in the plane.

"And that's the end of the list."

"So what do you think you've accomplished?" Manoling asked.

"Wait," Ronnie said. "Now I have a list of questions. Shall I read them?"

"You might as well. I haven't anything else to do."

"These aren't all the questions," Ronnie said. "I didn't put down the big question: Where is Rafael now? Or the questions that only Rafael could answer, like where he was planning to go that day. I put down questions that maybe we can find answers to."

"Go ahead," Manoling said. "Never mind the buildup."

"Who brought back Rafael's diving things? Did anybody see anyone bring them back? Have you asked Engracia and Teresita and Hsu?"

"No. They would have told us if they had seen anyone."

"But would it hurt to ask them anyhow?" Ronnie said. "And here are some more questions. Did Rafael ever go diving with anyone besides Charles? Did he really intend to go diving that day? If he didn't, why did he take the diving stuff? If he did, why didn't anyone in Baler see him?"

"I thought you weren't going to write down the questions that only Rafe could answer."

"Maybe we ought to think about them," Ronnie said, "even if we know we can't answer them. You want to *do* something, don't you?"

"Thinking isn't doing."

Ronnie said, "That's a matter of opinion. When you're as old as I am——"

"Any more questions on your list?"

"Why was Celia afraid to talk to you?"

"I know one reason already. Her father didn't want her to go out with Rafe. He's Chinese, and they keep their daughters shut up until they get married. He doesn't like our free ways."

"But you thought she knew something she wouldn't tell."

"Oh, I don't know. I was mad at her that day."

"But you could talk to her again," Ronnie said. "Couldn't you?"

"If she lied before, she'll lie better this time. But I'll try. I'll try anything that makes a little sense. What else?"

"This isn't really a question. I think we ought to go back to that airstrip."

"Nobody was there but us, Ronnie," Manoling said. "And you know that my mother told Charles not to take us there again."

"But Manoling, just suppose. Suppose for one minute. You only say, No, it's a nutty idea. But that was the easiest time of all for anyone to get near the plane. The plane was out in the open, all alone. We couldn't see it from where we were."

"But that place was empty."

"How can you be so sure? And if your mother knew we were doing it for Rafael, she'd let us go back."

"Let me see your list," Manoling said. He held out his hand for the papers and then studied them. Not looking up, he said, "I don't know why you're so interested. You never even saw Rafe."

The words hurt so much that for a moment she couldn't answer. But perhaps, she thought, he hadn't known he would hurt her. Anyhow, she would explain as well as she could.

"Anyone would be interested," she said. "And he's my cousin. And you think he's wonderful; so I'm sure

I'll think he's wonderful, too, when I do meet him. And I've seen you, and Uncle Frank, and your mother, and Charles. And this is a wonderful home. I wish I had a home like it."

"You have a home in the States."

"Oh, yes. I have a lot of homes. The apartment in New York. That's my mother's and my stepfather's. And my father has two houses in Florida. And my school is like home, too. That's four homes. But one is really enough. And I know that wherever Rafael is, he'd rather be here. So of course I'm interested."

"O.K.," Manoling said. "I'm sorry I said what I did. But as for your lists, I wish you hadn't made them. Reading them makes me feel I know less than before. I can't think of anything to do that will be any use."

# 8

# *Reconnaissance Patrol*

Monday evening Manoling yielded to Ronnie's persuasion and talked to the servants. They learned nothing.

Hsu was sitting at the kitchen table, with books and paper in front of him and a pencil in his hand. He looked up at them owlishly and said, "Doña Paz has asked me to use the cold ham tomorrow. But there's fried chicken."

"We aren't hungry," Manoling said. "We want to ask you a question. On that Saturday when my brother disappeared, did you see anyone bring his diving things and put them in the garage?"

"Bring his diving things? Someone took them? Someone has now taken them? I don't understand."

"He took them," Manoling said. "Who brought them back? That's what we want to find out."

"He took them? Then he brought them back."

Ronnie's heart thumped. Had Hsu seen Rafael come
back that day?

"You saw him?" Manoling asked.

"I didn't say that," Hsu said. "On Saturdays I always
go to the market. I have a mere bicycle to use. It takes
me a long time. On a Saturday I see nothing." He
turned back to his book, making a note on the margin
of the page he was reading.

"Well," Manoling said, "thanks for giving me so
much of your valuable time." Hsu gave a slow nod,
accepting these thanks, and Manoling opened his
mouth to speak again.

But Ronnie with a quick motion silenced him, and
led him out of the kitchen. "His time *is* valuable," she
said. "He's studying, isn't he?"

"Studying! Oh, sure; he's taking some correspon-
dence course from a college in Manila. But he could
answer a question without being so disagreeable about
it."

"He answered," Ronnie said. "I don't think he was
disagreeable. And think of his pies and his cookies and
his bread and his rice and that chicken tonight—what
is it called?"

"Chicken Valenciana. Do I dare go back and ask for
a piece of cake?"

Ronnie said, "No. Engracia and Teresita first." She
followed him to their rooms, which like the kitchen
were on the ground floor of the house, and waited
while he talked to them. She could guess what they
were saying by the way expectation slowly faded from
his voice.

"Teresita was away all that day," he told Ronnie.
"Engracia says the diving stuff was here all the time, as

everyone knows, and anyhow no one came to the house, for if they had she would have known it because she knows everything that happens here."

"Is that true?"

"Obviously, no. Because someone did come. She likes to think she knows everything that happens here. But there's plenty she doesn't know anything about. I've known that for a long time. And so," he added, "your list hasn't helped, has it?"

"There's Celia," Ronnie said.

Manoling said, "We won't learn anything from her, either."

He was right. They rode to the barrio Tuesday morning, under a clear sky and through a thousand mud puddles, and Ronnie got Celia out of the shop by refusing to leave the shop without her. Once more, penned in by the truck, the motorbike, and Ronnie and Manoling, Celia said she had not seen Rafael on that Saturday or for a long time before. There were no tears this time, but a defiant stubbornness.

Some thought nagged at Ronnie during this interview, something she wanted to say or to ask, but it was a vague thought that she could not shape into words. She had to give up, uneasy and dissatisfied, when Manoling gave up his questioning and let Celia go back into her father's shop.

Tuesday night, Charles returned. He agreed with Ronnie—though not, she realized, for her reason—that another visit should be made to the mountain airstrip.

However, it was Ronnie's reason, the possibility that Rafael's watch had been placed in the plane at that lonely spot, that persuaded Doña Paz to let Manoling and Ronnie go with him.

"As soon as you think it's dry enough," she told Charles. "For the others who use the field must come from farther away, and they will not dare come soon after the storm. It will be safest then. And you remember that we must take special care of Ronnie. Her mother warned us that she seems to enjoy getting into difficulties."

Ronnie had smiled at hearing the permission to go, and she kept the smile on her face. But she did not enjoy hearing that she enjoyed difficulties. She did not think it was either kind or just. She felt that older people enjoyed misunderstanding her. But she kept this feeling a secret, letting it gradually submerge under the excitement of plans for another flight to the airstrip.

They went on Wednesday afternoon.

Standing beside the plane at the south end of the strip, the three of them paused for a long look at the surrounding jungle wall, at the mountains rising near them on the east, at the distant mountain ridges they could see at the north and west, at the deep and empty blue sky. At this moment Ronnie's hopes sank down into the ground. Someone here had put Rafael's watch on the plane? Never. The someone would have had to drop out of the sky, as they themselves had done. And that had not happened, on that other day when the plane stood alone on the strip.

But Charles said, "There has to be a trail leading to this place. The ground had to be prepared by men on the ground. They had to have a way of coming and going. Perhaps this place is used now only by planes. As a transfer point. But perhaps it isn't, and that means there's still a trail, a good one, for us to find. We ought to find it even if it's grown over with vines.

"You two go that way," he pointed left, "and I'll go the other. You know what to look for, Manoling. You've done some mountain work. People can be clever at hiding the beginning of a path, you know."

They started behind the plane and proceeded close to the green wall.

At Charles's advice, Ronnie wore slacks and long sleeves. Sweat soon glued her shirt to her back, but she was grateful for protection from the sharp blades of the coarse grass and from the thorny vines stretching out from the jungle.

She could see Manoling's eyes searching for an opening among the trees, and she helped him pull at vines wherever he thought they might hide an entrance through the wall. He was conscientious but his heart was not in what he was doing. A trail might be found, but what difference would it make? "If Rafe was near enough to put his watch in the plane, or send someone to do it here, why didn't he follow the watch? Or come with it? Or at least write a note? This isn't the way we're going to find him."

Ronnie talked to him, trying to raise his spirits, trying, too, to raise her own.

She said, "This is worse than a stone wall, isn't it? You could break a hole in a stone wall and climb through. Or make a ladder and climb over it."

He nodded, kicking aside leaves.

"This wall is alive. I can almost see it growing. I can smell it. It has a strong, weedy smell. Sort of dank and creepy. I think it's very mysterious."

He said, "There's nothing mysterious about the

smell. It comes from the wet leaves we're walking on. Maybe the place is creepy because it's full of creepers, bejucos and lianas."

"So it's a joke to you," Ronnie said. "But it scares me."

"I've told you before, Ronnie. It's being scared that hurts you. If you panic, you're lost."

Ronnie said, "I'd panic."

"Maybe you would and maybe you wouldn't. I mean that. Rafe and I used to talk about it. Everybody wonders if he'd panic. Nobody knows until it happens to him. Rafe wouldn't panic. I'd bet on him. And I think I'd bet on you. You have more sense than most girls."

Surprise at the compliment left Ronnie speechless for a long time.

They were more than halfway around the strip when they met Charles. "Any sign of a trail?" he asked them. But they had found no path into the jungle and he had found none.

"Then there's a last possibility," he said. "I didn't want to try it without telling you where I was going."

He led them through the cave-like hollow in the forest where a plane had been concealed, not stopping until he reached the stream at the back. "Wait here," he told them. "I'm going to follow this for a way and see what I find." The noise he made in wading diminished quickly and then was lost entirely in the sound of the running stream.

When they heard his voice again, he was speaking from behind them, and they turned to see him silhouetted at the entrance to the hollow. "Hi!" he called. "Come and I'll show you. I found another place where you don't have to do so much wading."

To their secret delight it was Charles himself who had earlier missed the beginning of the trail. It was in the southeast corner of the strip, where a rocky projection of the mountain rose only a few yards inside the jungle. He lifted a tangle of vines for them to scramble under, and then they held the vines for him.

Here was the same stream again, the clear, shallow water running over stones. "Be careful," Charles said. "Too easy to fall here and break a leg."

They waded slowly downstream over the uneven, slippery stones. Plants and bushes and young trees grew thickly along the water's edge on each side for a distance that Ronnie guessed must be at least two hundred feet. Then they came to a muddy, open bank, and here it was plain that they were on a trail that was in present use.

"These tracks are mine," Charles said. "There aren't any others. Rain washed away the last. But you can see that someone's been using a bolo and keeping the vines and bushes cut back."

"Who?" Ronnie said. "People from the plane? Who are they?"

"You want me to guess? If this were one of the southern islands, Mindanao, for example, it would be an Indonesian plane. From a base in the Celebes. Up here in Luzon—well, there's too much choice. Japan, and the two Chinas, Red China and Taiwan, and also Hongkong. Smuggling is an old Oriental custom."

"They're not smuggling anything big," Manoling said. "It's a good trail. But nobody carries anything bulky down a trail like this."

"That's right," Charles agreed. "This isn't one of the places where someone is stealing timber." He had been gazing into the forest, where for some distance the trail could be seen. Now he turned. "Too bad it's so late in the day. I'd like to go farther than this."

"We'll have to come back," Manoling said.

"Correction," Charles said. "I wouldn't dare bring you back here again. Even if your mother agreed. You go first, Manoling. Then Ronnie. No, I'll have to come back alone." He followed Ronnie into the stream.

"And that's all we've learned from another item on your list," Manoling said as he helped Ronnie crawl under the vines at the edge of the strip. "A smuggled Swiss watch might be dropped here. But not Rafe's. Rafe has nothing to do with any of this. And it's as empty as the moon, except when a plane lands here."

"I know," Ronnie said. "But you aren't really sorry we came, are you?"

He answered with a shrug. Ronnie knew how he felt because she felt the same way. As he had said before, what was going on here might be important to a great many people, but it was Rafael who was most important to his family.

They got in the plane and strapped themselves in their places. The engines roared. Charles listened, watching his instrument panel. Manoling copied each move Charles made.

Only Ronnie was looking out of the plane.

She was looking, though for no special reason, toward the western jungle wall. It seemed darker and thicker than before, because now, in the late afternoon, the shade there was heavy.

Yet as she watched this wall that she believed to be impenetrable, a face appeared in it, such a face as she had never seen or imagined. It was small, so brown that it was almost black, wide-nosed, full-lipped, tiny-eyed, topped with a mass of frizzy gray hair.

She cried out and touched Manoling's arm.

He looked at her but could not hear her words, and when she glanced again toward the jungle, to point, the face was gone.

She wondered if she had indeed seen a face there.

And the plane was moving.

# 9

# Operation: "Ronnie"

Ronnie watched the family and listened as, at dinner that night, they talked of the airstrip.

She was silent. Except for one piece of information, she had nothing worth saying. And what she had—was it really information? Was it worth saying? Had she really seen a face? If she had, and if she said so, would anyone believe her?

"We'd better give that airstrip a name," Charles said. "I keep saying 'up there' or 'that place' and somehow it doesn't seem real."

"Call it Danger Valley," said Doña Paz. "And stay away."

Manoling said, "It didn't seem dangerous while we were there."

"That's right," Charles said. "It was peaceful enough today."

"Peaceful enough for what?" Doña Paz said. She looked at Ronnie. "I suppose you, too, say it was peaceful. But you should be warned of danger by your feminine intuition. I believe in feminine intuition. Mine is warning me."

Ronnie said, "It was very quiet. I felt safe." But with her mind's eye she looked again into that ugly, startling face.

What had she seen? A warning by her feminine intuition? No, surely it was real! But who would believe her?

"My name for it is still Danger Valley," said Doña Paz.

Manoling's father had been almost as silent as Ronnie. He asked now, "And you think you won't report this again to the Constabulary?"

Charles said, "I wonder. Do you think I should? They'll give me the same answer as before. They'll investigate when they have time. The trouble is that they have too many more urgent problems to deal with."

"But you're convinced it's been used recently?"

"Absolutely convinced. Something is coming in or going out. Illegally."

Frank Richardson said, "Coming in or going out or both."

"That's right. The same people could be engaged in smuggling in both directions. Drugs. Swiss watches. Weapons. Those coming in. And money, especially dollars, going out. The usual stuff."

"And any of it is dangerous," said Doña Paz, "to the person who discovers what's going on."

"But it should be discovered, Pacita," Frank said. "If no one will listen to what we know now, we must learn more. Charles can't promise you not to go back there."

"He can at least promise not to take the children. I should not have said that he could take them today."

Children! Ronnie and Manoling turned to stare at each other and then to stare at Doña Paz. Children! They were not children!

When the table had been cleared and Ronnie and Manoling were left there with Manoling's Latin book, Ronnie could see Doña Paz as she sat reading a newspaper. Children! The name rankled.

Abruptly Doña Paz stood up, throwing the paper onto a table. "Why do I look at it?" she said. "On the front page, graft and dirty politics, robbery and murder. More bombs stolen from Clark Air Force Base. And then on page two, the glitter—the receptions and the dinners and the birthday parties and the weddings —and often the same names that were on the front page in the stories of dirty politics. I can hardly breathe in such an atmosphere!" She went to the piano and opened it, saying, "This will be out of tune. That is the way it should be. To suit the world." She sat down and began to play.

Manoling raised his eyes from the book but did not turn his head to look at his mother. Frank and Charles, as Ronnie saw, were listening but pretending to continue their reading. Only Ronnie listened openly. There was a nervous chill running up and down her backbone. She had longed to hear her aunt at the piano, but she had never dreamed it would be like this.

In the wide, shimmering sleeves of her Philippine dress, Doña Paz was a green and black butterfly. But her music was not the light and airy music that might

suit a butterfly. It was jangling and harsh and tuneless
and angry. And then it changed, growing quieter, and
it upset Ronnie more. It was so sad that she hoped it
would stop before she began to cry.

Almost as if this hope had been spoken, Doña Paz
stood up, closed the piano, and went to her room.

And Ronnie forgave her for the word, *children*, and
was ashamed of being forgetful of the strain that Doña
Paz usually concealed from them so well.

And yet the name rankled.

Manoling pushed his books away and leaned his
forehead on both hands.

When he raised his head and said, "No more Caesar
tonight," Ronnie was not surprised. But his next words
did surprise her. He said, in a murmur that his father
and Charles could not hear, "It's a good thing she never
heard about our ride to Baler."

"Why?"

"Because she'd tell us not to go again."

"Do you want to go again?"

"I might want to go somewhere on the bike. And I
don't want to be told that it isn't safe for children to
ride on a motorbike. She's giving up about Rafe. I'm
not."

He leaned his head again on his hands.

Ronnie waited a little before she dared a question.
Then she asked, "Do you want to go where they found
the motorbike?"

"I don't know. Probably not. The Constabulary
searched there and didn't find anything. I couldn't
search there better than they can. Anyhow, I don't
think he ever went there. Remember?"

"You haven't stopped thinking he went to Baler?"

He rolled his head on his hands, indicating no.

There was a question in her mind and there was an idea beginning there, too, and also she wanted to raise him out of his discouraged mood. She put the question, the vague thought, and the wish together, and said, "Manoling, I'd like to see where Baler is on the map. Do you have a map?"

"I could draw you a map," he said.

When he made no move to draw anything, she said, "Well, will you, please?"

"Will I do what?"

"Draw a map that shows Baler." She pushed paper and pencil toward him.

He reached slowly for the pencil, but then quickly made a map with sketchy lines and threw the pencil down. "There," he said, and gave the paper to her.

She knew before she looked at it that it was not a good map, but she pretended to examine it carefully. She said, "I see Baler and Baler Bay. But where are we? Can you put a mark for this house on the map?"

He took the map, made a tiny square for the house, and pushed the map back.

"And where did they find the motorbike?"

He took the map again, this time marked it with an X, and looked at it, shaking his head impatiently. He said, "I suppose I'd better put in the roads. From here to Baler." He drew a line. "From here to the Cagayan Valley." He drew another line. "Now are you satisfied?"

The lines for the roads were almost straight, and Ronnie knew that the road to Baler and perhaps the road into the Cagayan Valley, too, had as many curves as a family of cobras. But she did not complain. Probably the directions and distances were fairly true, and no matter how much they wound, the road to Baler ran east and the road to the Cagayan ran north.

She asked, "Is there a road between Baler and X?"

"You mean a direct road?"

"Yes. To make the third side of the triangle."

He looked at her with surprise. "Are you kidding? That's all solid mountains covered by solid jungle."

"How am I supposed to know that?" Ronnie asked. "I'll put them on the map." She made a series of peaks, in rows, to fill in the open space. "There. Solid mountains. I'll imagine that they're green, for solid jungle. And now——" she shoved the paper toward him.

"Now what? You want something more?"

"Of course. Where's 'that place'? Our airstrip?"

"I don't know," Manoling said. "Ask Charles."

"I don't want to bother Charles. You can guess, can't you?" She pulled the map back and studied it. "It's near the ocean. I know that much. And north of Baler?"

"Here." He took the map from her and marked it with another X. "Are you satisfied now?"

She was more than satisfied. The cloudy thought in her mind had become clear as she looked at this map. It had become so clear that it was more like a light than like an idea. It was becoming so bright that it dazzled her and she wondered that no one else seemed to see it at all. She blinked her eyes and tried to control her excitement.

"Manoling, no one believes you about the diving stuff. Is that right?"

"You know it as well as I do."

"But I believed you. From the first. Now I believe

you more than ever. Do you know why? Look at this map! Really look at it."

"I don't need to look at it. I made it, didn't I? Are you crazy?"

"No," Ronnie said. "I don't think I am. But it feels that way. Look where you put that last X. Near Baler."

"Sure. Two inches away. But this is a map, remember? Two inches can be a lot of miles."

"Listen, Manoling, while I tell you something that happened this afternoon. I didn't tell you before because I thought you wouldn't believe me. Just as they wouldn't believe you about the diving stuff. If you see something but if other people think it doesn't make sense, they'd rather believe what they think than what you saw." She added, "And we're children, remember?"

"And you don't think you're crazy," Manoling said. "But you show all the symptoms."

"I tried to tell you right away, but the plane was making too much noise."

He shook his head. "Worse and worse!"

"Listen, Manoling. Will you listen?"

"I'm listening. I'm afraid to move. I'm listening the way that poor guy listened to the Ancient Mariner."

"I saw it from the plane. It was there and then it was gone. I yelled, but you didn't hear me. And I was wondering already if it had been only my imagination. But how could I imagine a face like that?"

"A face?" Manoling said. "A *face?* Where?"

"Looking right out of the jungle. A face and that was all there was of it. Like the Cheshire Cat, you know. Though it wasn't smiling. If you've heard about the Ancient Mariner, maybe you've heard about the Cheshire Cat?"

"Never mind about cats and mariners," Manoling said. "What about this face?"

"It was the ugliest face I ever saw. It had little eyes, but they were sort of pop-eyes, too, and it was black, and it had a lot of bushy gray hair, and it had a nose that spread all over its face, and it looked wild and fierce, and it was way up above the ground. It must have been about twelve feet tall."

"It was probably about four feet tall," Manoling said.

"I wasn't exaggerating!"

"It was about four feet tall but up in a tree, Ronnie. Do you know what you've described? You've described a Negrito."

"So you really believe I saw it?"

"Yes. I agree that you couldn't imagine it."

"Shall we tell Charles?"

"Not yet. Let me think."

Ronnie waited, watching him and his reflection in the polished wood of the table.

When he looked toward her at last he said, "How would you like a little ride on the motorbike? As far as the hangar? It's not too late to go there tonight."

"O.K. But what for?"

"To get a little fresh air. Isn't that a good enough reason?"

# ❋ 10 ❋

# *Theater of Operations*

"What do you know about Negritos?" Manoling asked, turning the flashlight on the hangar door and taking the key from his pocket.

"Not much. They're wild and they live in the jungle."

"They're wild and primitive," he said. "They get along well with Americans. Some Americans I've seen are wild and primitive, too."

"Enjoy yourself," Ronnie said. "Be my guest."

"I've been thinking hard about this Negrito you saw. Have you been really thinking?"

"No," Ronnie said. "I don't have to think about him. He and I understand each other without thinking. You just explained that."

He pushed the door open and they stepped into the hot still darkness. "Of course you know why we came here."

"Not for fresh air," Ronnie said.

"We're going to search the plane. Because maybe the fellow you saw was the one who put the watch in the plane."

This was what Ronnie had been thinking but hadn't dared to say. "Yes!" she said. "Maybe!"

"Go ahead, Ronnie. Women and children first."

She climbed into the plane and he followed.

They made a careful search and found nothing.

They made a second search, as complete and thorough as the first, and again found nothing.

"But he could have been bringing something," Ronnie said. "And he got there too late. He looked disappointed."

"You weren't sure you saw anyone, and now you say he looked disappointed?"

"Yes," Ronnie said. "I do." She repeated, "He looked disappointed." She was sure now that she could remember the eyes rolling and the mouth opening. "Your brother would recognize this plane, wouldn't he?"

"Sure. If he saw it. That's one thing the orange paint is for. And he knows the size and shape. He'd recognize the sound of the motors, too. I do. When it's near enough."

He jumped out of the plane, and Ronnie jumped after him. For a few moments they stood there in the shadowy hangar in silence, the flashlights shining aimlessly at the floor. To Ronnie her idea still seemed sound. But was Manoling letting discouragement overwhelm him? She waited for him to speak.

"So we didn't find anything," he began at last. "That means we don't have anything to show anyone. That means they aren't going to believe any Negrito put the watch in the plane. But I know you believe it. And I want to believe it. I want to believe about the disappointed look. I want to believe that Rafe——" His voice trembled, and he stopped.

"We want to believe it and we do believe it," Ronnie said. "We believe he's alive. We believe he's somewhere near that strip. We believe that Negrito tried to get a message to us once. And he did. The watch was a message. But it wasn't a good enough message, or we didn't understand it. We believe he tried again. Today. And got there too late for anyone to see him except me. So it's my fault——" Now her voice trembled, but after a moment she continued. "And we believe we ought to try to find him. And that means you and me. Because nobody else is going to believe what we believe."

"Yes!" Manoling said. It was almost a shout. "Let's get out of here before we melt."

Outside the hangar the night now seemed chilly and Ronnie began to shiver. But it was excitement that kept her shivering all the way back to Topside.

As they reached the top of the stairs, Manoling said, "Look, Ronnie," and pointed beyond the verandah rail. Far away in the valley was a tree filled with fireflies. This sparkling and fantastic sight, like an escaped piece of fairyland, must be, Ronnie thought, a sign of good fortune in their search for Rafael. But she did not dare mention such a superstitious idea to Manoling.

Some of her excitement must have shown in her face, for Doña Paz, who had returned to the sala while they were gone, looked up from her book and said, "Manoling, you are tiring Ronnie too much. You two are livelier than fleas. Come here, Ronnie, please." She took Ronnie's hand. "Yes. Cold. Nervous. Manoling, you are younger than Ronnie, but you are bigger and this is your country. It is your duty and it should be your pleasure to protect her. Ronnie, you must go to bed and get a good sleep. I shall send Engracia with something hot to drink."

Ronnie and Manoling glanced at each other. Then Ronnie said, "Yes, Doña Paz," and went obediently to bed.

She drank the hot drink, too, which was chocolate, but with a different and delicious flavor that she could not analyze. She tried to obey also by going to sleep.

It was like her first night in this house. The more she tried to fall asleep, the wider awake she felt.

She had wanted to talk longer with Manoling. She had wanted to look again at his map.

For a long time whenever she closed her eyes, she saw the Negrito's face peering from its leafy background, and that would start her mind running again from one question to another about him and about Rafael.

If only he had appeared one minute earlier! Then all the questions might have been answered.

She knew when the rest of the family went to bed. She hoped they were sleepier than she was.

By one o'clock the image of the Negrito began to give way to a picture of the bowl of fruit on the buffet in the dining room. She was hungry.

When another hour had passed, she was very hungry.

There was also the map on the dining-room table. If she got up she could look at it again. She could satisfy two desires together.

The world outside was bright with moonlight. None came under the wide eaves directly into the house, but the house was not dark. She had no trouble in moving silently along the corridor and across the living room. In the dining room the table shone softly.

It was empty. There was not a paper on it. Perhaps that was what she should have expected.

She was even more surprised to find the fruit bowl empty, too.

However, she knew that a whole bunch of bananas, red ones, was hanging from a hook downstairs near the kitchen door.

Moonlight reached the stairs, but the kitchen was very dark. She had to turn on the light there so that she could find a knife.

Everything was neat and shining. The hum of the refrigerator emphasized the quiet. She tried to get a knife without making a noise, but the drawer stuck and everything rattled as it opened. But she made no other noise and the hum came to an end and the whole world seemed hushed and she was the only person anywhere who was awake.

She cut a banana and sat down on the stairs while she ate it. The air was warm and deliciously fragrant. The banana, too, was delicious.

The second banana was almost as good as the first.

A third? She pondered dreamily and decided against it.

Yawning, she put the knife on the table and carried the banana skins to the trashcan.

The yawn became a gasp when she lifted the cover. Here were the loose papers that had been lying on the dining-room table.

She gathered them up, dropped the banana skins onto the newspaper lining the can, which was now otherwise empty, carried them to the shelf beside the sink, under the brightest light, and began going through them.

She was slow and careful. They were a large and untidy handful, for Manoling had cleared out his notebook that evening. Ronnie looked at both sides of each paper.

She went through the papers twice, but didn't find the map.

She looked into the trashcan again to make sure that she had left no papers there.

There were none.

She was still adjusting the newspaper lining after looking beneath it, when Manoling's voice spoke behind her.

"What's going on here?"

She jumped, and turned to face him.

"Is this a scavenger hunt, Ronnie?"

She said, "Where's that map you made for me?"

"I don't know. I left it on the table."

"It's gone."

"Who cares?" Manoling said. "It wasn't a good map anyhow. I can make you a better one if you want one to keep. I'll make you four or five so that you won't have to get up in the middle of the night and look in garbage pails for one. I'm hungry. Are you?"

"I just ate two bananas."

"I want more than bananas," Manoling said, and he opened the refrigerator.

When they went up the stairs, their four hands were loaded. While he got paper and pencil and began to

draw, she made him a monster sandwich. Then he ate
as he drew, mumbling with his mouth full about the
details he was including. It was sure to be a better
map; she had seen that in the first line he made.

When it was done, he signed it, *Manuel Richardson,*
with large and fancy initial letters, and he stood up to
present it to her with a formal bow. Then he dropped
back on his chair, groaning, "I ate too much! All your
fault, too!"

Ronnie paid no attention to him. She was studying
the map.

"What's so fascinating about that map?" he asked at
last.

She answered him with another question. "How far
is it from the airstrip to Baler?"

"You know I had to guess about that," he said.
"Why?"

"Oh, Manoling, you must know why I want to
know! The trail from the airstrip goes south. Maybe it
goes to Baler. You must know what I'm thinking."

"The trail starts south. Maybe it hits a trail that goes
east and west. Maybe that strip is forty or fifty kilometers from Baler."

"And maybe it isn't," Ronnie said. "And maybe the
trail doesn't turn east or west. East it could only go to
the ocean, anyhow. You think Rafael went to Baler."

"And what are you thinking? That we ought to go to
Baler and look for a trail going north?" He got up.
"Wait. I just thought of something."

He crossed a corner of the dark sala and vanished in
the corridor between his room and Rafael's.

In a few moments he was back with a roll of papers.
It was thick and more than a yard long, tied with a red

and blue striped necktie. "Rafe's maps," he said. "If he's got one with Baler on it——"

Ronnie pushed the dishes to one side and Manoling placed the roll on the table and untied it. Together they unrolled it, and stood side by side, holding the corners down, looking at the top map.

"Manila. No use to us now," Manoling said. "You let your edge roll over this way and we'll look at the next one."

The map of Manila rolled itself away, revealing the map beneath. "It's pretty," Ronnie said. "Mountains! Is this the one?"

"No. It's Mindanao. The big southern island. Where the carabaos have no hair, that's the reason they're so bare—— No, wait. Hold your side." He spread the top map out again and then let the two roll up together.

He and Ronnie bent over the third. But at once he said, "No. Samar and Leyte. Next, please."

And so they went through the whole roll, and found the map they wanted on the bottom.

"At last!" Manoling said. He leaned the loose roll of the other maps against a chair, and he and Ronnie gave all their attention to the map under their hands.

"I see Baler," Ronnie said. "The town and the bay. And where would this house be?"

Manoling's finger hovered and then settled. "Right here. And here's the road through the mountains to Baler. And now let's look for trails. Dotted lines."

"There are a lot," Ronnie said.

He nodded. "Too many. And the map isn't new and trails can change and maybe these weren't more than guesswork to begin with. But at least we're sure there are trails." He added, "Of course I knew there had to be trails. There are always trails. All the mountain people have to have trails."

"There isn't any road, is there?" Ronnie asked.

"Up into those mountains? Even the road to Baler hasn't been there very long. It wasn't finished when this map was made. See? 'Road under construction.' People had to go to Baler by boat."

"Where is the airstrip? Those clover-leaf islands aren't on the map, are they?"

"No. Too little." Again his finger hovered, this time longer, and it came down with less certainty. "I don't know. We'll have to ask Charles."

"What's that you have to ask Charles?" said Charles's voice. "And what are you doing here at this time of night?"

Ronnie's sidelong glance met Manoling's glance. They understood each other. She would let him do the talking.

He said, "We were hungry. When I went down to the kitchen, there she was. Then we began arguing about where that place is up in the mountains. Danger Valley, if you want to call it that."

"I don't especially," Charles said. "Give me a pencil, will you please, Ronnie? I'd rather call it Doubtful Valley, or Happy Valley, or Valley of Desire, or Smugglers' Roost. Danger Valley is so melodramatic." As he talked, he leaned over the map, his eyes moving, estimating distances.

"That's Baler under your hand, isn't it, Ronnie?" he said.

"Yes," Ronnie answered. But she didn't move her hand. She moved closer and used her other hand to point. "Would the airstrip be about there?" she asked.

The area was much nearer Baler than the spot to which Manoling had pointed.

"Very good guess," Charles answered. He made a small circle. "I didn't measure it exactly, but it's in or near that spot. Now you two had better clean up here and then go back to bed. Before you wake your mother, Manoling."

"We'll be careful," Manoling said. "We'll hurry, too."

"Ronnie? Back to bed and back to sleep."

"I'll go back to bed," Ronnie said. "I'll try to go to sleep."

"Honest but cautious," Charles said.

Ronnie looked up at him. She said, "Honest people have to be cautious. I've learned that from experience."

Charles laughed. "I'm willing to agree with you. Well, you'll get moving?"

"We promise that," Ronnie said.

Charles laughed again. "You think that's a safe promise, do you?" He was smiling as he went back to his room.

"Listen, Ronnie," Manoling whispered. "Why did you ask me to mark where that strip is when you knew better than I did?"

"I didn't know. I pointed where I wanted it to be. And don't whisper. Whispers are really loud."

"All right," he said, this time in a low voice. "Now tell me what you're hiding under your hand."

She lifted her hand and showed him. It was a very faint question mark in pencil just above the symbol on the map indicating the town of Baler. She said, "Rafael must have put it there. And why was this map on the outside of the roll?"

Manoling said, "Because he had been using it last."

This was what Ronnie, too, believed.

# ❧ *11* ❧

# *Losing the Initiative*

"While we wait," Ronnie said, "tell me more about the Huks."

She and Manoling were slowly finishing a late breakfast. It was too early for them to start to Baler. They intended to make a casual departure, as if their plans were unimportant and time made no difference to them. They didn't want to worry Doña Paz. They didn't want Doña Paz to stop them.

"What's the difference," Ronnie said, "between Huks and guerrillas?"

"The Huks are guerrillas but not all guerrillas are Huks."

"And some guerrillas are good?" Ronnie asked. "Like the guerrillas who built that airstrip during the war?"

"That's right," Manoling said. "You're learning."

Ronnie made a face. "I appreciate the compliment but I don't deserve it. I'm all mixed up. Or I've got the guerrillas all mixed up."

"Guerrillas are always all mixed up and they get people all mixed up. That's true. Confusion everywhere. That's what they want. They melt into the mountains, they melt into the jungle, but that's not all. They melt into a town, too, so that you don't know who's a guerrilla and who isn't. When you know you don't know anything about them, then you're beginning to understand them. No kidding. I'm serious."

"Then I'm making a perfect beginning," Ronnie said. "In the war with Japan, the guerrillas were good. Is that correct?"

"That's correct. They were part of the Resistance. Guerrillas are against the government, and when the government here was Japanese, it was good to be against them. But now the government is our own, it's Filipino, and it's bad to fight against it."

"Are the Huks Communists?"

"Some of them are and some of them aren't. The Reds got into lots of guerrilla bands during the war, and when the war was over, they kept on fighting against the government. Rafe says this happened in lots of countries. It happened in Malaya. It happened in China and the Reds won. Rafe says something like it happened in France, too. He says the Reds always take advantage of trouble. They watch for a weak spot and attack there."

Ronnie nodded. She knew a little about Castro's Cuba, and it fitted with what Manoling was saying.

But now he was talking about Rafael. "He'd never join the Huks. That's a crazy idea. He hates them."

"Do you think the Huks are using that airstrip?"

"I think they would if they could." He glanced at Ronnie's plate. "I can't make my breakfast last any longer. But it's still too early to leave. What shall we do?"

"How about some Caesar?" Ronnie asked.

He slumped in his chair. "That's always the first thing you think of."

"Why not?" Ronnie said. "This morning it fits just right. You'll act bored without trying and you can think of going on a picnic to get away from Latin."

He agreed, but without joy, and went to his room for his book.

Doña Paz did not stop them.

On Rafael's motorbike they bumped over the broken gravel road, passed through the small barrio where Celia lived, even glimpsed Celia and her father at the shop door talking to a customer, turned onto the mountain road, and went through the mountains, reaching Baler at about one o'clock.

They had traveled slowly from the time they started down out of the mountains, watching for any place where a trail met the road.

But I wouldn't know one if I saw one, Ronnie thought.

And Manoling, stopping the motorbike at the edge of the town, said almost the same thing. "I saw plenty of paths between the rice paddies and vegetable gardens. I suppose any of them might lead to a trail. But how can I know which one? We won't go straight into town on the main road. We'll go around the edge of town and see what we find." He turned the bike to the left. "Unless you're too tired to walk."

"I'm too tired to sit and bounce any more," Ronnie said. "Walking will feel good."

Pushing the bike between them, they left the road and started along an unpaved, muddy lane.

Here the houses were smaller; they were like the houses in Celia's barrio. They stood on stilts and had walls and roofs of shaggy brown palm leaves. Around them and under them small naked children played— until they saw Manoling and Ronnie. Then they stopped playing and stared, especially at Ronnie, until she felt like an animal in a circus parade.

Quite soon they found two paths leading off northward, one a little to the west and the other a little to the east. Manoling stopped to consider them. But it was rather easy to see that neither led farther than to some rice paddies.

When the muddy lane turned back toward the main road, Manoling halted under a big mango tree. "Now where?" he said. "Let's try to think and be wise about this. How about a sandwich? That bakery truck over there makes me feel hungry."

"Me, too," Ronnie said. "And it makes me feel at home. I remember that same truck or another from the same bakery last time we were here." She looked at the sandwiches she had taken out. "Chicken? Yes, chicken."

"Too bad you don't feel enough at home to know which way we should go now," Manoling said. Gloomily, he bit into his sandwich.

It was hot even in the thick shade of the tree. There was no breeze anywhere. Ronnie heard a rustling overhead, but a chirp now and then told her a bird was moving through the branches and not the first light gusts of a cooling wind.

The bakery truck started up and drove away.

A few people went in or out of a shop on the corner where the lane met the main road. They all stared at Ronnie.

"You're a freak in Baler," Manoling said.

"I know it already."

"They won't forget you. Too bad we're not looking for you. Everybody would remember you."

"How could I look for myself?" Ronnie asked. "I always know where I am even if I'm lost."

Manoling paid no attention to this nonsense. He said, "I could eat another. Couldn't you?"

She got out two more sandwiches.

Manoling yawned. He said, "Let's move before I fall asleep. We can eat while we walk along. We'll try the next side street."

But again they found only paths leading out to rice paddies.

At last Manoling followed one of these to one of the small dikes around the paddies, walked along that, and talked to a woman who was setting out new bright green plants.

There was a smile on his face as he returned.

"She says there's a trail that starts near the north end of Baler Bay, across the Baler River. But we'd need a boat to go there; so that's out. But there's one that hits the main road about half a mile before you get to Baler. I don't know how we missed it, but we did."

They walked the bike back along the road. Manoling didn't trust the woman's estimate of distance, or, in fact, his own ability to find a trail he had already failed to see. If they rode, he thought they might pass the trail again.

But approached from this direction, the trail was easy to see. It had been hidden from them before by the bamboos growing along a small stream. Also, a ditch now full of water hid the place where the trail and the road met.

Manoling looked at this water and then at Ronnie.

Their plans for the day had been indefinite. In fact, they had not really made any plans at all. They had agreed that they must return to Baler and try to find a trail that might lead toward the airstrip, but they had not talked of what they would do if the trail was found. Now they had to decide. They looked at each other questioningly.

"Is this the Rubicon that I see before me?" Manoling said. "Would Caesar cross it? Would you?"

"It looks like a long way across the valley before we come to any mountains. And we don't know how much farther it would be to that place."

"It might be fifteen kilometers. It might be thirty. Charles made that circle on the map plenty big. Thirty kilometers is about twenty miles."

"Twenty miles!" Ronnie said. "And you told me that ten miles on a mountain trail might seem like fifty on a road. And it's two o'clock."

"Nobody ever said we'd try to go all the way to the strip. But I'd like to go far enough to find something to show that Rafe went this way."

"What could you find?" Ronnie asked. "Do you

think he dropped pebbles, like Hansel and Gretel? Do you think he expected you to follow him?"

"You don't understand, Ronnie. People live near these trails. There are some little barrios. Maybe somebody saw him. Rafe and I look enough alike so that if they see me, they might remember him. So what do you think?"

"Well," Ronnie said, "it isn't really the Rubicon. We can come back across it."

"That's right," Manoling said eagerly. "We can go for an hour and then start back."

"Whether we learn anything or not?"

"Yes. I agree."

"What about the bike?" Ronnie was still hesitant.

"If the trail gets too bad for us to take it along, we'll hide it. There'll be plenty of places to hide it."

"What about getting it across the ditch?"

"I'm not worried about getting the bike across the ditch," Manoling said. "I'm worried about getting *you* across the ditch."

That decided Ronnie. "I'll do my own worrying, thank you," she said. She sat down on the edge of the road and took off her shoes and socks and rolled up her slacks.

The bike was soon a great nuisance. In some places the trail was very narrow. Bamboos and bushes seemed to reach out maliciously for the spokes of the wheels. There were mudholes to dodge and there were small streams that couldn't be dodged. At last Manoling said, "We could go twice as fast without the bike. I'm going to hide it in the next big clump of bamboo."

"Good riddance," Ronnie said.

She had already given up taking off her shoes and

socks for the puddles and streams they had to ford, and now she thought she had been silly to remove them for wading the ditch beside the road. Thinking of the road, she glanced back at it, for surprisingly it could still be seen although they had come a long way between rice paddies and across marshes.

There on the road, which was raised like a causeway across the low valley, stood her old friend the bakery truck. It did not seem to be moving, and she saw it again when she glanced back a little later. More engine trouble, she thought.

Without the bike they were moving more than twice as fast. Soon, too, they came to deeper streams, across which they could not have taken the bike without a boat or a raft.

There was little shade. The sun beat down and perspiration ran into Ronnie's eyes. Mosquitoes hummed around her head. Yet she was not so miserable as perhaps she should have been in such circumstances. She was actually enjoying herself.

Manoling told her stories, to match the story of Hansel and Gretel, which he had asked her to tell him as they started on the trail. He told her why dogs wag their tails, and how monkeys can be captured with a coconut, and how tricky and wise the turtle is, and why the kalaw screams in the night.

Meanwhile, although the mountains remained distant, the foothills were coming near.

Then, abruptly, the trail arrived at the low, soggy bank of a wider stream and began again across the stream on a bank that rose several feet higher. "At last," Manoling said, "we're beginning to get somewhere."

A bamboo raft was tied to a tree on each bank by a rope long enough to let it travel back and forth. There was an overhead rope, too, for guidance and propulsion, a clever though primitive arrangement. "But modern, too," Ronnie said. "Self-service."

They ferried themselves quickly to the opposite side and clambered up the muddy slope.

To their surprise they saw near the trail ahead a small round thatched hut, hardly more than a roof.

"Wait," said Manoling, and went toward it.

In a moment he was back again. "Empty for a long time," he said. "Come on."

Ronnie glanced at her watch.

"I know," he said. "Fifteen minutes more. Then we turn back." He repeated, "Come on."

It was easier traveling on this higher, drier ground, and Manoling went faster. Ronnie found it harder and harder to keep up. She tried; she didn't want him to know that she had begun to feel tired.

However, he must have noticed, or perhaps he was tired, too. He said nothing, but when they came to a field of young sugarcane, he stopped and cut a piece for each of them to chew.

"Fresh energy?" said Ronnie. "Thanks."

He nodded and said again, "Come on," although the fifteen minutes had ended. She did not mention the fact.

Back in the rice fields they had seen a few people in the distance, plowing or planting. Here they saw no one working. Corn was growing here, as well as the cane, and there were other things Ronnie could not identify. But if people were near, they concealed themselves as Ronnie and Manoling went by.

Now they came to another stream, really a river, swifter as well as wider and deeper than any they had crossed before. This one they cross in a *banca,* a heavy dugout, placed here for a ferry. Manoling pointed to the banks on each side, where the mud had been churned by many feet. It was obvious that this stream was frequently crossed. He murmured, "We must be close to where they live. Stay behind me, but stay near."

They climbed the steep bank—here they were coming to much higher ground—and entered a field of cane with purple stems and green leaves as high as Ronnie's head. The trail after they passed through this cane turned westward, and there they saw a group of a dozen or more houses, snug and brown in the thick greenness at the foot of a low mountain.

"Negrito houses?" Ronnie asked.

"Negritos don't build houses. These must be Ilongots."

"Who are they?"

"Tricky people. Sometimes good and sometimes bad. But at least they don't take heads any more. Or at least Ilongots around Baler don't take heads. When that happens once in a while these days, it's farther north, in the higher mountains, where they think the Constabulary can never catch them." He thought for a moment. "It might be better if I go alone to talk to them."

"Shall I go back and hide in that sugarcane?"

"No. I don't want you out of my sight. Come along until I tell you where to wait."

When he had left her, she watched him anxiously. Dogs had already begun to bark at them and were soon running out to meet him. They circled him in mad excitement, but did not attack. Next came the children, and after them came those she knew must be adults, though the tallest was inches shorter than Manoling. It was easy for her eyes to follow him, except when now and then he disappeared behind a hut. He apparently was going through the whole settlement, with all the inhabitants gradually surrounding him.

He was there exactly twenty-one minutes, which to Ronnie felt like an hour, before he started to return, leaving men and women, then children, then dogs, group by group, behind him. Halfway to her, he raised both arms and waved them. Nearer, he lifted one hand with fingers spread in a V.

She started toward him. Victory! What did he mean? Surely not that Rafael was here?

"No," Manoling said when she asked the question. "But he went past here on this trail. A few of these people speak Tagalog. They'd talk to each other, and then only translate a word or two, but I heard enough. Rafe was seen. I know it."

"They remember him?"

"I told you he looks like me. And he stopped here and asked questions. About where this trail goes, and who uses it. He was alone. And he went on."

"But didn't come back?"

"If he did, no one here saw him."

"Manoling, where does the trail go? Did they say it goes to the place we know?"

Manoling shook his head. "They say it goes up into the mountains. They say the mountain people use it. Maybe they know more than that. Maybe they don't."

"They must have told the same to Rafael."

"I think they did. And he went on. So . . . what do we do now, Ronnie?"

"We don't know how far away he is from here."

"That's true."

"And it's late. It's going to be dark before we get to Topside. No matter how much we hurry."

"That's true, too."

"So you know what we ought to do, Manoling."

"Yes. We must go home, and get help. And come back here tomorrow."

"Yes, we must," Ronnie said. "I know you want to keep on going. But we shouldn't."

The return trip seemed only half as long. It seemed hardly any time before they reached the clump of bamboo where Manoling had hidden the motorbike.

They were certain it was the right place. Manoling had tied two branches of bamboo together to conceal the opening. The string had been cut, but part of it was still there.

The motorbike, however, was gone.

# 12

# Combat Patrol

Ronnie said, "We can't get back to Topside."

"There's always a way," Manoling said. "We just have to choose the best way and the quickest."

Ronnie said again, "We can't go back." She was surprised by the steadiness of her voice. It didn't show at all what she was feeling.

"We'll hitch a ride," Manoling said. "Don't be silly. It's easy. It's safe. You're with me. Anyhow it's safer hitchhiking here than in your country."

Ronnie said, "Do you think the people that took the bike are going to let us go home?"

"The people that took—what do you mean? It's stolen, that's all, and the people that took it are as far away as they can get. So forget about them for now, and let's get going."

Ronnie didn't move. "I know who took the bike. And you do, too."

He took her arm and then let go, staring at her. "What are you trembling about? And what do you mean, you know who took the bike and I know, too?"

"You'd know if you'd only think. Think, Manoling! *Think!* Remember that somehow the bike was stolen from Rafael, too. Of course the same people took it."

Manoling was thinking. She could see it. He nodded slowly.

"Manoling, that bakery truck—I'm sure it's that bakery truck. I think the bike is in that truck right now. I think if we went back to the road, that bakery truck would come along and offer us a ride. Or come along and run over us."

"I'd like a ride in a bakery truck," Manoling said. "I'm hungry." But his heart wasn't in this attempt at a joke. "You keep talking about a bakery truck. What bakery truck?"

"Don't you remember? We saw it two or three times on our first trip to Baler. We saw it again in Baler today. And the last time I saw it, it had stopped on the road, where they could see us starting on this trail. They were watching us. I know they were. I believe I was frightened then, but I thought it was silly of me."

Manoling didn't answer. He was still thinking.

Ronnie said, "I'm not going back to the road. I mean it. You'd have to drag me."

"We can try to find another trail to Baler," he said.

"But that woman said we'd need a boat for the other trail. And it might take hours to find the other trail. Manoling, we have to do what you wanted to do."

He understood what she meant. He said, "It's going to get cold in the mountains as soon as the sun goes down. And we haven't any food. When they got the bike they got our sandwiches, too."

"Would those Ilongots let us have some food? You have some money, haven't you?"

"A little," Manoling said. "Maybe we can get some camotes and some rice." He added, "There's something else I can ask them for, too."

"We've agreed?" Ronnie asked.

"We've agreed."

"Then let's stop wasting time," she said.

At the Ilongot settlement Manoling hired the brightest boy he could find to take a message to Baler, to be sent to Charles. Then he and Ronnie went on, eating the balls of rice the people had given them.

The trail now was much steeper. They talked little. When Manoling did speak, it was to express his worry about the message to Charles. Had he said enough? Had he said the right thing? "We're safe. Exploring that place." Would Charles understand? Would Charles see that Doña Paz didn't worry?

"Charles will understand," Ronnie said. "If he gets it. Maybe that's worth worrying about."

But Manoling was certain Charles would get it. It was to go through the Constabulary, and they would find him, wherever he was. And the boy had been promised a bonus if the message went through.

"Then stop worrying," Ronnie told Manoling. "It's a good message and you didn't have room to write more. You were lucky to find that little scrap of paper and that pencil stub in your pocket. Of course Charles will understand. Of course Charles will keep your mother from worrying. If anyone can."

They were now high enough on the foothills to see that the mountains north of them were very near. But

the shadows of the westward mountains were nearer
yet. Quite soon the sun would disappear. Too soon.

It was still daylight, however, when they forded another wide stream and heard the dogs of another settlement barking.

On their second visit to the other Ilongot settlement,
Ronnie had stayed with Manoling, and this time he
told her to come with him again. "If you're not afraid.
You did fine before."

"I think it's fun," Ronnie said. "I like their questions.
Yes, I'm white all over. No, I'm not a boy. I'm a girl
although I'm wearing slacks." She continued as they
came in sight of the houses, "And I want to be near if
they give us something to eat. This place looks bigger.
Not so poor, either. Maybe they'll give us more."

There were more houses and many were quite large
and all were set among taller, older coconut palms, and
there were many big, old mango trees on which hung
golden fruit.

But the people were hostile. The small naked children who ran out with the dogs were called back and
pulled into their houses. Men and women seen in the
distance had vanished before Ronnie and Manoling
came close. Only the barking, snarling dogs stayed
near, in a cowardly circle that traveled with the two
strangers. Manoling wisely had picked up a stick.

Fortunately one older girl's curiosity kept her peep-
ing around a tree long enough for Manoling to come
within speaking distance, and then she lingered, half-
hidden, talking with him.

The waiting needed all Ronnie's patience. She tried
to keep her face from showing anxiety and at the same
time tried desperately to understand the expressions

on the girl's face and on Manoling's. There was not a single spoken syllable that meant anything to her. She did not even know which one was asking questions and which was answering. She thought that perhaps they were talking of nothing but her own freakish self, for the girl could not turn her eyes away from their examination of Ronnie's face and clothing.

When Manoling stopped talking and took Ronnie's hand, saying, "Come on. Act happy and carefree," she felt exhausted. She wondered if her weak knees could carry her away.

She wondered also if the dogs or if the people would pursue them. When she turned her back, her backbone was like soft jelly, quivering as she felt a hundred pairs of eyes boring into her.

She did not feel secure again until the village was so far behind that the last sound of the barking dogs had died completely away.

"That girl wouldn't tell you anything?" she said.

"She was only interested in you."

"She hadn't seen Rafael?"

"According to her they never see anyone. I don't know why she lied. Of course they see people. It's plain that there's plenty of travel on this trail. Trails don't stay open if they're not used. People further up the mountains go to Baler to sell and to buy. If this had been market day in Baler, we'd have seen a lot of people."

"But if the people in that village run and hide," Ronnie said, "then they wouldn't see anyone."

"They don't run and hide from the mountain people that use the trail. Those would be other Ilongots and Negritos. No, there's some special reason why they ran and hid from us." He added after a moment, "And I don't like it."

"You think it's something about Rafael?"

"It could be. I don't know. Maybe not. Maybe it was you. She asked if you were a ghost, or an evil spirit. Maybe I should have left you out of sight. They're certainly afraid of something. Do you think anything happened here to Rafe?"

In the last ten minutes daylight had faded rapidly. The mountains around them looked darker and higher. The air was suddenly much cooler.

Ronnie shivered. "Don't be so gloomy, Manoling. We're sure that Rafael is alive, aren't we? Maybe he isn't far away. Maybe we don't have far to go. Let's not get discouraged. And let's go faster while we can."

# ❀ *13* ❀

# *Obstacle:*
# *Rugged Terrain*

Daylight continued to fade, but before it was gone, they came to a division in the trail.

Right or left?

The trail to the left was plainer, wider. It was the more traveled trail. But the trail on the right led more toward the ocean.

They chose the right fork. "It's right to go right," Ronnie said. It was surprising how high her spirits were.

Fortunately for some distance yet they walked over grassy mountainsides. They knew they could not move at all in the jungle at night. Jungle is dark even in the daytime.

When the sun was gone, there was a moon to light their way. Ronnie said, "I wish I had a newspaper. I could read it by moonlight. I've heard of doing that but I've never done it."

"You want to read the headlines about us? 'Mysterious disappearance of Manuel Richardson and his cousin, Veronica Stewart, follows earlier disappearance of Rafael Richardson.' "

"My newspaper," Ronnie said, "is going to say, 'Brother finds long-lost brother.' Cheer up, Manoling."

"Cheer up, the worst is yet to come? It probably is. It's going to get darker and colder. And we're both going to get hungrier."

"I don't care!" Ronnie said. "This is exciting. This is adventure. I don't want to be anywhere but here."

"You'll get your wish," Manoling told her. "It's going to be a long, long time before you're anywhere but here. We're going about one mile per hour. When we're going fast."

But gradually his spirits rose a little and hers sank; they reached about the same level. Wearily, doggedly, Ronnie followed Manoling, watching the dark ground, where the thick shadows made every step treacherous.

Suddenly Manoling stopped. "This is where we have to give up for tonight. See ahead there? The path goes into that forest."

They were on the crest of a hill, not far from the forested peak Manoling was pointing toward. Ronnie looked up at it and then looked at her watch. It was ten minutes to eleven.

She was too tired to think of how far they had come or where they might be. She was too tired to wonder about tomorrow. She did not even know, now, that she was hungry. She only knew that she was glad they were going no farther that night.

The tall grass was coarse and very sharp; it was of no use for making a nest to curl up in. But at one side of the path there was a narrow stretch of softer weeds. Here they lay down, head to head, pulling the weeds over them for warmth.

"We can watch in opposite directions," Ronnie said.

"Don't bother about watching. Try to sleep. No one is coming. We haven't passed anyone; the trail is empty. Anyhow, with my ear to the ground, I'll hear anything moving. If I'm asleep, it'll wake me."

An ear to the ground, Ronnie thought. Moonlight bright enough for reading a newspaper. Now she knew from experience what these words meant.

Listening, with her ear to the ground, she fell asleep.

When she waked, it was very dark. The moon had set. She was cold and she was wet—not damp but really wet. It was dew, she decided, for the sky was clear. She sat up, shivering.

She could make out Manoling's sleeping figure. She did not disturb him, but got to her feet and moved away. With his ear to the ground, would he hear her?

No. He didn't move.

She was stiff as well as cold. Her legs ached. Cautiously she moved farther away, around a curve in the trail, and began some exercises to drive the soreness out of her muscles and to warm herself. "Live and learn," she told herself. For the first time in her life she was willingly doing what in her boarding school they called physical jerks.

By the time she felt comparatively comfortable, except for her empty stomach, the sky had begun to grow light. She set about making herself a little tidier.

There was not much she could do about her dirty,

wet clothes. If a stream had been near she could have immersed herself, clothes and all, and she would have come out cleaner and not much wetter. Having no stream, she gathered dew from the grass, taking care not to cut herself on the blades, and washed her hands and face. Her hair would have to wait until she could borrow Manoling's comb; she thought he had one in his pocket. Her own had gone with the motorbike.

"Ronnie!"

It was a cry of alarm, and she hurried to show herself.

"Hi!" she said. "I've been up hours and hours. I wish I could say that breakfast is ready."

"Why didn't you wake me?"

"You were sleeping like a baby."

"I pity any babies that have to sleep like this." He sat up. "I'm sore all over."

"Don't tell me. I know. Manoling, lend me your comb? Then I'll go ahead. When you can finally stand up, it will do you good to run to catch up."

She had nearly reached the place where the trail entered the forest before he overtook her. In the meantime the sun had come up, too quickly it seemed to her, turning the dawn clouds yellow and gilding the edges of the dark eastern mountains and then suddenly appearing from behind them. It was beautiful, but it made her feel a terrible loneliness. She didn't let Manoling guess how glad she was to see him.

He said, "I never knew girls were so tough."

It was a compliment she knew she didn't deserve. She said, "I had plenty of sleep. I bet you watched and worried. I bet you didn't sleep much. Did you?" She repeated, when he didn't answer, "Did you?"

"I slept a couple of hours."

"Because you felt responsible for me. And I was sleeping because I felt safe. What would you like for breakfast? I'd like bacon and eggs. Scrambled eggs. On toast. In the middle of the plate. A big piece of toast on a big plate. With pieces of bacon all around the edge."

Manoling said, "I'd rather have fried eggs."

"Why don't we have both?" Ronnie said. "This is nothing to argue about."

"Fried eggs, scrambled eggs, boiled eggs, hard or soft. I'd even eat *baluts*."

"What's that?" Ronnie asked.

"Your mother never told you about baluts? Has she forgotten that she was born in the Philippines? You ought to know about baluts. Duck eggs with half-grown baby ducks in them. Very nourishing."

"Oh, I'm sure," Ronnie said. "Delicious, too. What about big yellow ants spread on bread and butter? I've heard of that. Some place in England, in the country, way off from civilization."

"We could probably find the ants. But not the bread and butter."

Now they entered the forest. It was like walking into a dark house on a bright day. At first they had to concentrate on following the trail. Gradually, however, as their eyes adjusted, they saw more and more details of the trees and the smaller plants all around them. Manoling now and then showed her where dangling vines had been cut to keep the trail open. Sometimes he pointed up to where, far, far above, a ray of sunlight could be seen slanting into the top of a tree.

The angle of these rays told him that the trail continued to take them in the right direction. The cut vines proved that men had recently used the trail. "Wild pigs use the trail, too," Manoling said. "But they don't carry bolos to cut the vines."

Wild pigs and wild men, like Negritos, surely liked the trail, Ronnie thought, better than she did. It was steep and stony. It climbed up and down, but she realized that it was steadily taking them higher all the time. She clutched at roots or branches to help herself over the bad places. Her clothes had never dried out. Sweat soaked them now as dew had done earlier.

It was about noon when they emerged from the forest for the first time. The path ahead ran for a while along the top of a mountain ridge covered with the coarse kogon grass. The sun's vertical rays were burning hot. It was different from the moist heat of the jungle, but equally oppressive.

Ronnie was very tired. She could see that Manoling was very tired, too. But they plodded on. Strangely, she was less hungry than she had been earlier in the day.

They stopped once where a gap between mountains to the east gave them suddenly a glimpse of the ocean, while to the west Ronnie counted seven mountain ridges fading with distance from green to blue. There was a strong wind blowing. The mountains and the forest seemed as immense as the sea and the sky, and she and Manoling were the only people in the whole world.

They descended into a rocky gully with a swift stream at the bottom. Along the stream there were small trees and a lot of bamboo, and at the top of the gully on the other side the great trees of the forest began again. Manoling had been talking about a lunch of bamboo shoots and the young fiddleheads of ferns, two things they had already eaten that morning, though without much satisfaction.

But here in the gully, while they were looking for bamboo shoots, they were lucky enough to find some ripening wild bananas. The bunch hung down inside a thorny thicket and was several yards from the trail, and so had not been plundered by birds or people. With great care and not too many scratches, Ronnie and Manoling gathered a feast for themselves.

When they went on, they had new energy and courage. "Maybe the airstrip is only an hour away," Ronnie said, clambering behind Manoling up the side of the gully. "Maybe not even an hour. Maybe Rafael is just on the other side of this little hill."

"Save your breath," Manoling advised. "This little hill is a mountain." But his voice was as eager as hers.

The trees of the mountain forest were gigantic. The trunks were enormously thick, and they spread out toward the ground to give extra support for their immense height. All seemed to be reaching as high as they could for the light and the open air of the sky.

The forest was quiet. If there were birds, Ronnie did not hear them. Sometimes she heard rustlings near the trail, and she was startled; she was especially afraid of snakes. But the only living creatures she saw, except of course Manoling, were butterflies.

It was surprising to see butterflies in the gloom. There were some with transparent wings that Manoling called ghost butterflies, but to Ronnie they all looked ghostly, whatever their color, pale blue or red

or orange or brown, in their silent flight among the
trunks of the great trees.

It was not long before they could see light through
the thinning forest ahead. They did not think this
could be the airstrip, so near to the last open, grassy
stretch, but they moved eagerly, more quickly, forward.

Then Manoling abruptly stopped, motioning to Ronnie to stay behind. He went on alone toward the sunlight and stood a long time before he beckoned to her.
His finger at his lips warned her to be silent.

Half hopefully and half fearfully she looked past
him.

She saw a wide, grassy area, rising to the left of the
path and falling away to the right. From where she
stood, looking out as through a narrow door, she could
see neither the top nor the bottom of the slope. But
she could see most of the path as it crossed to vanish
far away into another jungle wall.

At several places, however, a break in the line of the
path showed where there must be a hollow in the hill-
side.

Manoling put his hand on her arm, holding her
back. "Wait!" he murmured. "Quiet!"

From one of the hidden curves where the trail disappeared, a man emerged. Only the head and the
upper part of his body could be seen; the rest of him
was hidden in the tall grass. Even at this distance the
colors of his printed shirt were bright against the green
grass.

Another man followed him, and then another, and
another . . . In astonishment Ronnie counted seven.

Manoling drew her back into the forest. "We'll have

to hide. At least until we see who they are. It's lucky we weren't the ones to get out into the open first."

Near the edge of the forest there was always more undergrowth than farther inside, and Manoling found a place where they could sit with enough comfort, hidden yet able to see the trail.

They had long minutes to wait, even after they began to hear voices. Ronnie grew more tense as each second passed. It seemed to her that surely her nerves would send out a message of alarm that would turn all seven pairs of eyes to the small leafy opening behind which she watched.

But the first man arrived and passed without a glance in her direction, and the others were equally unaware.

Numbers One through Five wore printed shirts of vivid colors. They were empty-handed. Six and Seven were burden carriers. Each had a pole on his shoulder with a suitcase at each end of it, so that Ronnie saw moving past her peephole a suitcase and a man and a suitcase, and then a suitcase and a man and a suitcase. Six and Seven wore cotton knit shirts soaked with sweat, and had cloths tied for sweatbands around their heads.

The men were not talking steadily, but with a few words now and then. Ronnie did not expect to understand them, and she did not try.

The sound of the voices was lost quickly in the forest hush, but Manoling did not risk moving until several minutes more had passed.

When he got to his feet and stretched, Ronnie quickly did the same, watching him and waiting for him to speak before she dared a word. But he did not speak. He made a gesture indicating that they were to proceed along the trail as before. He started and she followed.

He stopped only when they had crossed the grassy area and were inside the forest again.

"Who were they?" Ronnie asked.

"I wish I knew."

"What were they saying?"

"I wish I knew that, too."

"You couldn't understand them?" Ronnie said. "I was sure you understood them. I thought that was the reason you decided to stay hidden."

"No. It was because I didn't understand them. I think they were talking Chinese. I think the first five men are Chinese, but I'm not sure. It isn't always easy to know. There are a lot of Filipinos with some Chinese blood, and South Chinese have darker skin than North Chinese. I think these men are South Chinese, but——" He paused, thinking.

In a moment he continued, "I really ought to follow them, but now I want more than ever to go on. If one of us could follow, and the other——" He paused again, this time smiling and shaking his head. "Don't look so scared, Ronnie. We'll stick together."

Ronnie didn't say that she wasn't afraid. She was. At the thought of going alone in either direction, her heart had dropped into her stomach.

Now again the trail climbed steeply. Getting over the slippery rocks took all their attention.

There was nothing new in this part of the jungle, nothing that Ronnie hadn't seen or experienced already that day, yet after a while she began to have a new feeling about it. Something had changed. She kept looking behind and to each side, seeing nothing and wondering what she expected to see.

Or did she see something? Something that was there and then was gone? Something ahead of them? Or behind them? Some spirit of the jungle that was watching them?

Her hair was soaked with sweat and so were her clothes. Sweat dripped from her elbows. Nevertheless, a chill crept up her backbone and stirred her scalp. She was disgusted with herself. Had seeing those men stolen all her courage?

She was glad that Manoling didn't notice her nervousness.

Then Manoling halted so abruptly that she almost ran into him. Peering around him she saw the tiniest man she had ever seen. Because the trail rose sharply and gave him extra height, he and Manoling were face to face.

He wore only a G-string. He was very black and he had woolly gray hair. He was smiling but he remained very ugly. And he was surely the man that she had seen from the plane two days before.

Now she was sorry that Manoling had never noticed her nervousness. She would never be able to make him believe that she had felt this Negrito's stealthy companionship as they traveled through this part of the jungle.

# ❊ *14* ❊

# *Concentration of*
# *Forces*

On level ground the Negrito could easily have walked upright under Manoling's outstretched arm. His body was slender but muscular, and it was streaked with gray that Ronnie learned later was a combination of dirt and ashes.

He carried a bow that was taller than he was. A couple of arrows and a knife, invisible to Ronnie then, were stuck through the G-string behind his back. But by no means invisible was something looped and tied to the G-string at one side. She looked and disbelieved and looked again and believed and then in horrid fascination kept looking. It was a dead snake more than a yard long, with light spots dappling its dark glistening skin.

Ronnie listened anxiously as Manoling and the Negrito talked. They did not understand each other quickly, speaking only a few syllables at a time and each of them thinking over what he heard and replying slowly. But at last their talk came to an apparently satisfactory end.

The Negrito turned and walked forward along the trail. Manoling followed him and Ronnie followed Manoling as usual. She glanced beyond him whenever she could to see again that small figure in the lead. He was even dirtier behind than before, with dried mud clinging to his buttocks and occasionally dropping off. He had obviously been squatting in some muddy place, perhaps while waiting for them.

Ronnie reached around and found dried mud clinging to the seat of her slacks. There was no reason for her to feel superior to the Negrito. She was as dirty as he was.

As she drew her hand away, her finger caught in a long rip. In the jungle, she thought, clothes were a nuisance. Some other thought, too, stirred darkly in the back of her mind, but she could not bring it forward to see what it was.

The Negrito's feet were sure and quick. She and Manoling had to hurry to keep up, and she had really no breath for talking, but she used some to ask, "Where's he taking us?"

"Wait and see."

She also asked, "Is that a snake?" and got the answer, "Of course. For supper. Delicious."

After that she was silent.

But she could feel in Manoling a new excitement and a new impatience. Feeling this, she shared it.

The trail climbed higher. There were places where it was as steep as a ladder, where a ladder would have been much easier to climb. The Negrito went over such places as easily as he traveled on level ground.

At last they came to a smooth and level path again. Here, after a few steps, the Negrito stooped, pulled aside some large-leaved branches, and vanished. Crouching, Manoling and Ronnie followed.

Although the entrance was hidden, there was another path here, very narrow but plain to see, running diagonally away from the main trail. It led to a small open space among the trees, where the forest roof was as thick as ever but the undergrowth had been cleared away. Ronnie saw a thin feather of smoke rising from an almost invisible fire on the ground, and beyond this she saw a shelter of palm leaves supported on crooked poles.

Manoling was already running toward this shelter.

She was not far behind, and she halted beside him at a sort of platform. She looked down at the figure lying there. She knew that it must be Rafael.

Yes, he was tall; he was very long and thin. His clothes were of a light brown cotton, a tough cloth for hard wear, as Ronnie knew. But shirt and trousers were incredibly wrinkled as well as torn and stained.

He did not recognize Manoling. His eyes were open and his head was rolling from side to side, but he was not looking at anything. When Manoling put a hand to his face, it did not stop the rolling or make the eyes look at him. Manoling whispered, "He's burning up. Feel his skin."

She touched Rafael's hand. It was indeed burning and very dry. He retched as if to vomit, but nothing came.

"Malaria," Manoling said. "He had it last year. They

told him to be careful or it might come back." Then he pointed at Rafael's right leg.

In the deep shade she had to look carefully to see that between knee and ankle Rafael's leg was tied to a crude splint with strips of cloth. The cloth matched what was left of his trousers.

"It's broken," Manoling said.

She nodded. Of course. She knew that without being told. "But we've found him!" she said. "We've found him!"

"It isn't going to do him much good if we can't get him out of here fast. He has to have medicine. He doesn't know me! Did you see that?" He put his hand again on his brother's face and bent over him. "You're going to be all right now, Rafe," he said. "We'll get you home as fast as we can."

The Negrito had squatted beside the fire, and now Manoling went and squatted beside him. They talked as before, slowly, but at last reaching an understanding. Ronnie waited near Rafael; she felt helpless, now, and useless.

Manoling stood up and came over to her. "This trail goes on to the airstrip," he said. "A plane landed there today. But this fellow doesn't want me to go up there. It's a plane with black and yellow on the wings and the fuselage."

"That's Charles's plane. He got your message."

Manoling nodded. "So I'm going up there, of course."

"And leave me here?" She tried to keep the wail out of her voice but did not quite succeed.

"You can come with me," he said. "Not because you wouldn't be safe here, but because they're probably

more afraid of you than you are of them. And Rafe
will be all right for a little longer. They've been good
to him."

"They?" Ronnie asked.

"The family. They're all around us. Probably three
or four looking at you right now. Scared to death." He
glanced once more at his brother, and then said to
Ronnie, "Let's move. The sooner we start, the quicker
we'll arrive."

They had some distance yet to go, but the trail was
the easiest they had traveled. And when they came to
the stream, it was almost like coming home. They
stepped into the water.

At the same moment they heard the plane's engines,
first one and then the other, sputter into life.

They splashed recklessly through the water and
pushed through the underbrush at the corner of the
strip, only to see the plane rising into the air.

There were tears in Ronnie's eyes. She said, "Why
couldn't we be sooner? Why did we have to be just
one minute too late?"

"Because we're lucky," Manoling said. "Believe me,
we're lucky! Because that isn't Charles's plane."

"But——"

"Yes. It's painted like his. The pattern, the stripes.
But the color isn't quite the same. His is more orange.
And it's a different kind of plane. Do you think I don't
know the sound of Charles's plane? I'd recognize it
with my eyes shut."

"Then whose plane——?"

"I don't know," Manoling said. "But remember the
men who passed us. And this explains why our Negrito
friend didn't want us to come up here."

Ronnie dropped down on the ground. "So what do we do now?"

He had no answer ready.

Ronnie put her folded arms on her knees and put her head on her arms. She was so glad to sit down that the hard grass stubble felt comfortable. It was now late in the afternoon, and the sun's heat was pleasant. She was content to let Manoling think for a while.

However, it was she who spoke first. "It wasn't Charles. But do you think Charles will come?"

"It's possible. We knew it was possible. That's why we hurried up here to get help for Rafe. But now I think maybe we ought to try to get to Baler. Rafe's going to come out of that fever and feel better, but he'll still be awfully sick. His leg—that's probably pretty bad, too."

"It won't get dark for another hour," Ronnie said. "If Charles did come, he could get help a lot faster than we could."

"I know that. Ronnie——"

"What?"

"One of us ought to stay here. While the other goes to Baler."

"I was afraid you were going to say that," Ronnie said.

"I ought to go to Baler. I could go faster. Especially alone. Safer alone, too. If someone is watching for both of us."

"Suppose *you* fall and break *your* leg?"

"I'm not going to," he said. "Ronnie, you'd be safe."

"Sure. Safer than you, I guess."

"You could stay here until it begins to get dark. I'll tell the Negrito to come to meet you. You can wade down the stream while it's light enough for you to see, and he can meet you where you come out of the water. He knows his way in the forest at night. Don't worry about that."

"That's not what's worrying me," Ronnie said. She stood up. "My legs feel like spaghetti."

Manoling didn't ask what was worrying her. He said, "Why did you have to mention food?" He looked at his watch. "Don't wait too long, Ronnie. Promise."

That was an easy promise to make, for who knew what too long would be? She promised. "Now I'll hold the vines," she said, "so you can go under."

"Thanks," he said. "And I promise to get to Baler as fast as I can. I won't even stop for a sip of snake soup to speed me on my way." He crawled into the under-brush, and then, halfway through, turned back. "You're sure too, aren't you, that this is the right thing to do?"

She said, "I'm sure."

When she could hear him no longer, she dropped down on the ground again and put her head on her arms. She was glad he hadn't asked her if she was afraid. Perhaps he knew the answer and didn't want to hear it.

She shivered. The wind did not reach into this cor-ner of the strip, but the late afternoon sun was losing its heat. Her damp clothes felt horrid.

Snake soup! She shivered again. How hungry would she have to be before she ate anything like that?

She dozed a little, woke with a start, looked at her watch.

Manoling had been gone for five minutes.

Now in the lonely quiet she began to hear small,

stealthy sounds. There were rustlings. There were tiny clicks. Something fell softly and then there was a silence. Then the rustlings began once more. There were louder clicks, like the snip, snip, of a tiny pair of scissors. The rustlings increased, and then paused, and then recommenced.

She did not close her eyes again. But each time she looked around herself there was no creature to be seen. No snakes were gliding toward her. In the grass near her she did not see even an ant. Probably, she thought, the rustling was the wind.

She got up and walked a short distance along the edge of the strip and back again to the corner. Her legs felt stronger after a little use. But inwardly she quivered.

Slowly more minutes went by, and more. The sun had little farther to go before it disappeared behind the darkening mountains in the west. Twilight then would be short. She should be on the path, meeting the Negrito, before it was dark, or she might never find the path at all. Twilight outside the jungle would be night inside it.

If Charles didn't come in the next three or four minutes, she would have to start. The sun always went suddenly at the last.

Why hadn't she suggested that she stay on the airstrip all night? The idea seemed sensible and desirable now. Why hadn't she thought of it before?

The Negrito was already on his way to meet her and to lead her along a trail darker than midnight. She knew that she had to meet him. Meeting him on the trail was not so frightening as not meeting him. In the jungle any human company was better than none.

Pythons hung by their tails from trees. They looked like vines that were everywhere. Manoling had told her that. They would drop on a man and swallow him, feet first. "Shoes, too?" Ronnie had asked. "And socks?" It had been funny then. "The hinges of their jaws loosen," he had said, "and they can open their mouths wider than you'd ever believe."

She believed it now.

The rim of the sun touched the top of the mountain. The sun was red. A cloud streaked across it was black.

Ronnie turned away from the sunset to scramble under the thorny vines. They, like the rest of the jungle wall and the ground, too, had changed color in the fiery glow from the sky.

She was ankle deep in the cold water when she heard a plane. It came closer until the roar was very near. It went away. It returned.

She thought, This must be Charles! He's circling. Is he going to land? Will he land if he doesn't see me or Manoling waving to him?

Then she thought, This might be the other plane returning. Will they land? What will they do if they see me?

While she thought, she was moving. Now she was on her knees, hidden, but looking out through the underbrush. And the plane was already on the ground. It lost speed, turned, taxied toward her end of the field, turned into the wind, as Charles had done, ready for taking off. It looked like Charles's plane, but to her eyes the other, too, had looked like Charles's plane.

On the far side of the plane someone jumped to the ground. Hardly breathing, she watched the legs. They seemed to take forever to bring their owner around the front of the plane.

It was Charles. That curly fair hair, bright even in the fading light, belonged to no one but Charles. She recognized even the pattern of his shirt.

Shouting, "Charles! Charles!" she began to scramble and claw her way into the open. The thorns caught her hair and her clothes. Charles was there to help her before she got herself free. He pulled her upright and held her tightly by the arms while he looked down at her. "You're all right, aren't you?" he said. "Aren't you? What are you doing here? Where's Manoling?"

"I was waiting for you. We hoped you'd come. And you did!"

"Yes, I'm here," Charles said. "But where's Manoling? You two—you don't know—where's Manoling? Isn't he with you?"

"He started back to Baler. To get help. Rafael's leg is broken." Ronnie was half-choked with excitement, words trying to come too fast for her to speak, but she knew very clearly what she was saying. She watched Charles's face for his reaction. "He has malaria, too."

"What did you say?"

"He has malaria, too. He should get to a hospital. Fast. So Manoling is going to Baler. I stayed here waiting for you. You got Manoling's message."

It wasn't a question, but he answered it. "About an hour ago. I got here as fast as I could. Wondering if I was crazy to come. But everything is crazy today— what did you say? *Rafael* has a broken leg? *Rafael* has malaria? You and Manoling found *Rafael*?"

Now pride joined Ronnie's excitement. This was a

wonderful, unbelievable moment. But she made her answer as simple as possible. She said, "Yes."

He dropped her arms and thought for a moment or two. Then he said, "Now let me get this straight. Rafael must be in the jungle."

"Yes. A Negrito family has been taking care of him. We think the Negrito man put Rafael's watch in your plane." She had been the one to insist on this belief, but it was easy in her triumphant mood to give half the credit to Manoling.

Charles said something under his breath, and she did not understand. Quickly and more loudly he went on, "And you say Manoling started back to Baler? That means you came from Baler. I can see that; it's possible. How long ago did Manoling start?"

She looked at her watch. "An hour and five minutes."

"Let me think," Charles said. "There isn't much time before dark."

She waited in silence, watching his eyes move unseeingly as he thought.

It seemed longer, but it didn't take him a minute to make up his mind. "All right, Ronnie," he said. "Come on." He began walking toward the plane in long strides. "Manoling hasn't got far yet."

Ronnie had to hurry to keep up with him. "Where are we going?"

"To Manila, where I'm sure I can land after dark and get things moving. Hop in, Ronnie." He gave her a push up into the plane. "You've had about all you can take, haven't you?"

Ronnie said, "I feel fine." It was true. It was also true that she was suffering from hunger, weariness, weakness, dirt, insect bites, blisters, scratches, and perhaps more. But that didn't matter.

Charles flew his plane south first, following the trail as well as he could with the directions Ronnie had been able to give him, and circling low at several different times. He hoped that Manoling would hear the plane and understand that help was on its way.

Then he headed for Manila. Once he pointed down, and Ronnie saw the headlights of two lonely cars on a mountain road. She knew that it must be the road to Baler, and the marvel of flying impressed her more than it had ever done before. In a few minutes they had passed over ground that it had taken her and Manoling almost two days to cover on foot.

In Manila Charles kept her with him while he talked to men who would arrange help to bring Rafael out of the mountains, and she told her story again and again, describing the trail, the loss of the motorbike, the men who had passed them on the trail, the meeting with the Negrito, Rafael and his condition, and the trail's end at the airstrip.

Charles got milk for her, and sandwiches. She knew that she would always remember how good they tasted, but that she would never remember all the places she went to that night or all the men who questioned her.

The evening ended when Charles took her, still dirty and in her torn and dirty clothes, to the famous Manila Hotel, where they found a maid to help her bathe and go to bed.

# *15*

# *Character of the Enemy*

A rap on the door waked her. It was dark. Charles's voice called, "Ronnie!" He opened the door and switched on the light. He said, "It's early, but we're going to be busy."

He had a clean shirt for her, from the supply of fresh clothing he kept at the hotel for his frequent trips to Manila. Behind him came a waiter with a breakfast tray.

She ate while she dressed, hurrying to do both quickly. The shirt was of course too large, like Charles's pajamas, which she had slept in. But largeness was a good fault. The shirt covered a little the same dirty, torn pair of slacks that she had been wearing.

One glance in the mirror was too much. Her hair was clean and shiny and normal, but her face, though clean, was mottled and swollen with mosquito bites. She had known about them but she hadn't guessed how many there were.

Charles told her their plans as they rode to the airport. "The men I talked to last night figure that the plane painted to look like mine probably comes from one of the small islands off the north coast of Luzon. Those islands are like stepping stones from China. I'll show you later on a map.

"They figure, too, that the people up there may not learn right away that we know about their use of the airstrip. There's a chance that the plane will make another landing there. If it does, they want to trap it.

"So this is what they're going to do—if the weather is good enough, and here at least it looks good. They are sure they can land a plane up there and take off again earlier this morning than the other plane, coming from one of those little islands, could arrive. But from that time on, they don't want the airstrip used. They want it to look as empty as usual. So they will land some men to watch the strip, and they'll land a doctor——"

"To get to Rafe quickly," Ronnie said.

"That's right. It's easy enough to find that end of the trail. I've told them where to look for it."

"But they won't be able to take Rafe out that way?"

"Suppose that plane should return in the middle of a rescue operation? It's not merely the trap they're worried about. That plane may be armed. That wouldn't help a rescue operation. So they'll take Rafe down the trail to Baler.

"Now, how do you feel today, Ronnie? I'd like you

to go along as a guide, even if we get a good guide in Baler."

"I went up there once when I was hungry," Ronnie said. "I can do it again even better when I've had something to eat. It was a wonderful breakfast, Charles. Poor Manoling! Do you think he went back to stay with Rafael after he heard your plane?"

"We know he hasn't arrived in Baler. I'm sure we'll find them together. Then Constabulary men that are specially trained for mountain work will carry Rafe out of the mountains. From Baler he'll be flown here to Manila. And Frank and Doña Paz are probably on their way here now. They'll be at the hospital when he arrives. How does it sound?"

Ronnie thought it sounded fine.

Now she remembered to tell Charles about the bakery truck that she had seen so often. "The name was Nitapayán Sampaguita."

"It can't be Nitapayán," Charles said. "Tinapayán. However, you know it might be a fact that their truck keeps breaking down. There are such trucks. But don't worry. I'm not going to disregard any of your ideas. They can be too important for me to overlook them. We'll investigate, as soon as we know that Rafael is safe."

The rescue of Rafe went according to plan. It was slow but it was successful.

At noon of the next day Charles flew Ronnie and Manoling home and left them there, while he flew on to Manila. He returned to Topside just before dark.

They lingered at the table after finishing their supper, talking about Rafael and his rescue.

"I don't know how you two kids did it," Charles told them. "It's a hard trip even for men who are used to it. You had a lot of luck. You know that, don't you? And you showed a lot of good sense. And some bad. I suppose you know that, too."

"When did we show any bad sense?" Manoling asked. "Everything we did turned out all right, didn't it?"

"You could each have broken a leg, too. Or your necks——" But then Charles stopped a moment. "O.K.," he went on. "I won't say any more about that. Everything has turned out all right. Just as you say. You were reckless, you were playing with dynamite, but you got away with it. Perhaps Rafe would never have been found, if someone hadn't played with dynamite."

Ronnie said, "You were playing with dynamite, too, each time you landed on that airstrip."

Charles stared at her in surprise, and then laughed. "You're right. I'm as bad as you are."

"Or as good," she said.

"Or as good," he agreed. "But it was dynamite, and it still is, and we don't know very much yet about that dynamite. It can still blow us all up. We have a lot to learn. The doctors say Rafe is too weak to be questioned; they had to set his leg again, and he's under sedation. Those men that you two saw, probably talking in Chinese as they walked past you in the jungle, have vanished as if the earth opened and swallowed them up. The plane hasn't returned to the airstrip yet. I'd like to get my hands on the man that painted it to look like mine! Most people are not observant. If they saw it, they'd just think it was good old Charles flying around up there in the sky.

"And also, Ronnie, there's your mysterious bakery truck. Nobody in Baler had ever heard of any Tinapayán Sampaguita. And there isn't such a bakery in any barrio or town near this end of the road to Baler. So you've got something there, though I don't know what."

"Have they found the motorbike yet?" Ronnie asked.

"Didn't I tell you?" Charles answered. "Yes, they found it. They've taken it to examine for fingerprints and so forth. They found it almost exactly where they found it before."

"Planted," Manoling said. "To make it look as if that was where we disappeared. And planted by the same people that planted it before."

Charles nodded. "If it had been found before you were found, we would have believed what they wanted us to believe."

Manoling said, "You would have believed them again. But nobody would believe me when I said that Rafe had gone to Baler."

"Nobody but Ronnie," Charles said. "We'll thank you both as long as we live."

"And scold us both?" Ronnie asked.

They all laughed. "Probably," Charles said. "And we'll get tired of hearing you say, 'I told you so,' and you'll get tired of hearing us say—well, I don't know yet what we'll say too often. But in the meantime——" He paused and shook his head. "Sometimes words are weak." He paused again.

"But we're all very lucky," he continued after a moment. "We're all very happy. And remember—maybe we're not finished yet. So go to bed and be ready for tomorrow. How will a bed feel, Manoling?"

Manoling said, "I'm going to sleep too hard to appreciate it."

He was not yet awake when Ronnie got up the next morning. It was late. Charles had already left for Manila.

Engracia gave Ronnie her breakfast in the kitchen, cooking it herself, for Hsu had gone to do some marketing. She hovered around Ronnie, exclaiming in her own language at the insect bites and the scratches. Ronnie did not need words to understand that to Engracia she was a heroine. With or without words, Engracia, at least, would never scold her for her recklessness.

There was an idea in Ronnie's mind that she could hardly wait to tell Manoling. Time dragged until he appeared at last.

And then, she could see, he was in no mood for any talk. He didn't want to speak and he didn't want to listen.

Ronnie thought she knew why. He wanted to be in Manila. That was where something interesting might happen. At Topside this was going to be an ordinary dull day. He was clean and he had had a good sleep in comfort and he was going to have plenty to eat and he wasn't going to have to climb over wet rocks on a trail that resembled a waterfall, but today wasn't going to be as good as the days when he had been miserably cold, hungry, dirty, wet, tired, and worried.

Ronnie pretended to read for a while. She, too, felt the dullness of an ordinary day. She also felt that she and Manoling had been left outside the main stream of

events and that this was something they had not de-
served.

But there was one interesting thing that they could
do. In fact, the more she thought of it, the more she
believed that it must be done.

It was important for her to choose the right time and
the right way to tell Manoling about it.

After he had wandered in and out of the sala a
dozen times, he sat down and opened a magazine.
Ronnie watched him carefully with sidelong glances,
keeping her head down over her book. He was reading
no more than she was.

When he threw down the magazine, she raised her
head. Then she said, in the dullest tones she knew, "It's
been two days since we did any Caesar."

He answered with the groan she expected.

"We don't have to read the next part. We could read
something more interesting. Like the bridge he built
across the Rhine. Or his invasion of England." No one
could have guessed from her voice that these were
parts she did indeed find interesting. She added, still
in the same spiritless way, "My teacher says that
studying history helps us to understand what's hap-
pening today. Hitler wanted to invade England. He
didn't dare. You've heard of Hitler?"

Manoling said, "My brother says that the only thing
you learn from history is that nobody learns anything
from history." With the words *my brother* his expression changed; he seemed to come to life. But he continued gloomily, "Anyhow, I'll have to go back to
school. I suppose you can help me on weekends. If you
want to. And I don't know why you do." He got up
and went out to the verandah.

She waited a moment or two and then decided to follow him. She found him leaning against the rail, looking over the valley. Toward his school in Baguio? Toward nothing? She wondered briefly but didn't ask. It didn't matter.

She said, "What color is Celia's father's delivery truck?"

"I don't know. Who cares?"

"I care. Is it green?"

"I told you I don't know."

"You don't say it isn't green?"

"I never noticed. It could be any color. Not red. Or yellow. It could be green, I suppose. So what?"

"Because it's the same kind of truck as that bakery truck. Manoling, that first day when we saw Celia, I caught my shorts and tore them on a broken fender on that truck. And that time when we passed the bakery truck and it was stalled, that first time that seems so long ago, there was a man leaning against the fender and when we went past, he started to move away and then jerked back, just the way I did. Just as if he'd caught his pants. I can see him now, and the way he put his hand back. I thought he was reaching for a gun. But now I think his pants were torn and he was reaching to feel that tear. Because those two trucks are the same truck."

"How can they be the same truck? Lots of trucks have broken fenders. Plenty of trucks are green. And the bakery truck has the name of the bakery on it. Celia's father's has his name, and it says Kabundokan, Philippines, and it has pictures of cigarettes and Coke bottles."

"But maybe—please listen, Manoling, and please

think! Maybe those signs aren't painted right on the truck. Maybe they're on a separate piece that can be taken off and changed."

Manoling was staring at her. He said, "Let's see if they've brought back the motorbike."

But the garage was empty.

They had reached the top step on the back stairs when they heard a car coming up the hill. From the verandah rail they saw with wondering eyes that it was Li's truck, coming to them when they had given up hope of seeing it that morning.

The body of the truck was green.

For an instant Ronnie felt that her feet were fixed to the floor, that she couldn't lift them. But she could. She was following Manoling down the steps before the truck had drawn up near the kitchen door.

Manoling darted into the kitchen and she stopped at the door, seeing him pull out a drawer, reach into it, pull something out. A knife? No. A screwdriver.

Hsu, standing at the sink, turned his head and craned his neck. The reflection on his glasses made Ronnie see a face with two great round unhuman blanks for eyes. She felt a thrill of alarm, and again she felt fixed to the floor.

But again she was close behind Manoling when he jumped down the steps to the ground and went to the side of the truck.

"Look there," he said. "Screws at each corner and a couple between, top and bottom. No. Too big for this screwdriver. But the panel's removable. You're right. They can't turn it over, though. It rounds out." He went to look at the edge of the panel. "Look, Ronnie. I think both panels are here. They can put either one outside. And hide the one they're not using under-neath."

They hadn't noticed the driver and he must not have seen them when, with the truck between them, he had got out and had gone into the kitchen. Now they heard his running feet, and the slam of the truck door, and the motor starting, all in a second.

Ronnie, looking toward the cab, saw the driver's head project suddenly from the window, his neck twist, his eyes turn on them with such a glare of hatred that it was like a blow.

She knew what he was going to do. He was going to try to run them down. At least, she thought, the truck can't go sideways; while we're beside it, we're safe. She seized Manoling's arm as he started to move. "No! No! He's going to——"

The gears crashed and the truck jumped forward. The gears crashed and it jumped back toward them. Manoling pulled Ronnie back, but they had no time; the truck was too fast for them. They could never reach safety.

But the truck came to a jolting stop. The driver had miscalculated. He had driven into the cement steps. Crashing the gears again, he pulled away.

Manoling and Ronnie leaped up the steps that had saved them and got behind one of the big posts sup-porting the balcony. Here the truck could not reach them, but what else might the driver try?

There was a shout from the kitchen, and out came Hsu. To defend them? The outlandish words he was using were a new bewilderment to Ronnie, a new terror.

No, not to defend them. Hsu had a heavy suitcase

in each hand. He could not leap. He could not run. He scuttled, and the suitcases scraped on the steps. The truck was quivering in time with its motor, but it was stationary. Hsu pushed one suitcase into the cab, and then the other. Now he could jump, and he jumped in. The door wouldn't shut, but the truck started up.

Hsu looked back. Light flashed on his glasses.

And the truck turned the corner of the house. It was gone, except for the sound of the engine. Soon that was gone, too.

Ronnie sat down on the stairs with drooping head and closed eyes and began to tremble.

After a while Manoling spoke to her and she looked up.

"Can you shoot?" he asked. "Do you know anything about guns?"

She shook her head.

"I don't think they're coming back," he said. "But if they do come, we'll be ready for them. Engracia and Teresita can both shoot. Come up now and I'll give you a lesson."

It was better to move than to sit and shake with fear. By the time she reached the top of the steps she was nearly recovered. Soon her hands were steady enough to hold a gun as Manoling explained it to her.

"Remember that you don't have to hit anyone. All you have to do is shoot. And remember that we've had trouble here before. We're used to it. And anyhow they're not coming back."

When Charles arrived an hour later he agreed. "They're a long way off by now. And I'm afraid we're not going to catch them. Come with me and we'll get to the nearest telephone and report this to the Constabulary. But it's already too late."

When they were back at Topside again, he gave them news of Rafael. "Rafe is fine," he said. "And he's been telling us some of the things we wanted to know. He saw a truck unload several men at Li's store one night. That's what started him to thinking. They had suitcases. They seemed to be new arrivals. When he asked Celia about them, she began to cry and wouldn't tell him anything. And after that Celia was forbidden to see him.

"For a couple of months, when we thought he was with Celia, he was trying to learn more about that truck and those men. It was his vacation; he had plenty of time. He followed the truck to Baler. Twice he saw it standing, stalled, in the same place on the Baler road. He saw that a trail began there. And also they began watching him and following him.

"So he decided to see where that trail went."

"And broke his leg," Manoling said. "Did he tell you about sending the watch as a message? Or about taking his diving things when he left that day?"

"He hasn't told us everything yet. But those are things we understand well enough, don't we? The diving things were to mislead anyone who followed him —only it didn't mislead them. They followed and removed the motorbike and probably waited anxiously for him to return and wondered as much as we did about his disappearance. But Hsu! That wonderful cook! There's the real mystery."

Manoling said, "It must have been Hsu that brought Rafe's diving stuff back here."

"It could have been," Charles said. "We never sus-

pected him. His cover was perfect." He added, "But he
was right to run. We would have begun thinking of
him soon."

"You don't think he'll be caught?" Ronnie said.

"I think he's probably going to get away. I think
they probably had everything planned for escape if it
were necessary. He's probably too important for them
not to try to save him. But poor little Li—he'll be
caught. He's always been expendable. They blackmail
these local Chinese into aiding them."

"Who are *they?*" Ronnie asked. "You talk as if you
know."

"They?" Charles said. "They are agents from Red
China. As Manoling guessed the day you saw some of
them walking through the jungle. They are sent here to
stir up trouble wherever there's a chance of it. You've
heard about the Huks. And college students are easily
stirred up. And laborers. Wherever there's any dissatis-
faction, the agents go and make their promises. Promises are cheap, when you don't intend to carry them
out. And I'll agree that things aren't perfect here.
There's a lot for the government to do. Some of the
problems are very old, without simple solutions. The
agents look for the weak spots—it's an old story."

"He was such a good cook!" Ronnie said.

Charles and Manoling both laughed.

"He is a very clever man," Charles said. "This was a
very good place for him to be. He wanted to keep the
job. So he was good at it."

Ronnie said, "He must have found that map Manoling made for me. With the airstrip marked on it. That
warned him."

"I think he's had several warnings lately. He was getting ready to run."

Manoling said, "I'd like to know what he had in those heavy suitcases. A radio set? For sending messages?"

"Speaking of suitcases," Charles said, "your mother, Manoling, wants me to get you back to Baguio tonight. Do you have to pack anything? We ought to go soon."

Manoling made a face, but he went obediently to his room.

He was probably, Ronnie thought, already planning how he was going to tell all his friends about the rescue of his brother and about the airstrip and about the Chinese cook that was a Red agent and about the narrow escape when the truck driver tried to back into them. Manoling might not want to return to his studies, but there was more to school than studying.

But what was she going to do alone in this house?

"Ronnie," Charles said. "Ronnie, do you hear me?"

She nodded with her face turned away.

"He'll be home every weekend. And in a couple of days Rafe will be here. He's going to be convalescent for weeks. You'll like him, too. And he's as bad in English as Manoling is in Latin. How are you in English?"

"So-so." But she was really a little better than that.

"Well, even so-so is good enough to teach Rafael. How are you in math?"

"Terrible!"

"Then Rafe can help you. The Richardsons can accomplish anything, if they stick together. Aren't you delighted about the math?"

Ronnie made a face worse than the one Manoling had made. She said, "I'm extremely delighted."

"Do you want to ride up to Baguio and back? Then get ready."

Ronnie, starting toward her room, turned to ask a question. "Has Doña Paz found a new cook yet?"

"Ronnie! Are you hoping for another Red agent in our kitchen? I'm afraid that would delight you more than the math lessons."

"No! Never!" said Ronnie, but she could not help smiling.